FESTIVAL OF THE GHOST

João Morais has a PhD in Creative Writing from Cardiff University. He has previously been shortlisted and longlisted for the New Welsh Writing Awards, shortlisted for the Rhys Davies Short Story Competition, the Percy French Prize for Comic Verse, and the All Wales Comic Verse Award. He won the 2013 Terry Hetherington Prize for Young Writers. His short story collection, *Things That Make the Heart Beat Faster*, was published by Parthian in 2018.

FESTIVAL OF THE GHOST

JOÃO MORAIS

PARTHIAN

Parthian, Cardigan SA43 1ED
www.parthianbooks.com
© João Morais, 2024
Print ISBN 978-1-917140-16-4
Ebook ISBN 978-1-917140-17-1
Editor: Gwen Davies
Typeset by Syncopated Pandemonium
Cover design by Matt Needle
Printed by 4edge
Published with the financial support of
the Books Council of Wales
British Library Cataloguing in Publication Data
A cataloguing record for this book is available from the British Library.
Printed on FSC accredited paper

27 MARCH

1.50PM

I read somewhere that keeping a journal can help with the grieving process. Every time I have a thought about you, or something happens that reminds me of you, I'm supposed to write it down.

Well, today was meant to be the day of our final goodbye, so you were always going to be the only thing on my mind.

It was just you and me left in the hall. But I couldn't even, for the very last time, see your face and kiss you on the cheek. My silence was broken by a long, unpunctuated message I received from whom I assumed was the lorry driver. I stared at a ceiling light, like I always have to when I want to feel clean, doing what you and Mum used to call one of my funny little quirks.

But your casket wasn't even in a straight line. I needed the release, I needed to find its correct position. If I didn't then I couldn't be clean again.

I wheeled you until your casket was parallel with the back window. But then the flowers on top weren't in balance with the lectern, so I rearranged them to make sure the pinks and purples didn't touch. I looked down and I found myself clicking my fingers, trying to find the right pattern which would stop me feeling like there was a tumour growing in my head.

And in that second I noticed I was no longer alone. It was you.

I don't know how but you were stood at the lectern. You were dressed in black and your hair was up and your mouth was moving as if you were talking, but no sound came out. Then you stopped, and stared at the back of the hall.

I fell into a seat. You were in the casket. I had helped carry you in myself. The violence of what had happened to you was in there. But you looked so young. You were skinnier and smaller somehow, with a rounder face.

And I knew, right then, that I had seen you like this before.

Five years ago at Mum's funeral. You caught me sneaking in late and I had to stand at the back. You'd spotted me and welled up and you couldn't get your words out. And now I was seeing you go through it again.

And just like that you were gone.

I grabbed at the air where I'd seen you. I looked at the casket, at the flowers on top. I went to look inside, but the thought of what I would see made me cold and weak.

Outside there was a sea of people in black. I walked through the mulls and murmurs. A man with a big collar said sorry for my loss. The undertaker, Mr Sparrow – the same one we had for Mum – asked if I was ready to head to the wake.

But all I could say was, – I saw her. I just saw Alexis in the hall.

And all he could say back was, – I'm not sure you should tell anyone that at the wake, son.

I pushed past one of your friends in a yellow coat and went back in. The lectern was in the same place, but now it didn't look like it was aligned correctly with the wall, as if its position made the whole world wrong.

I shifted it over. But this made me feel like my body was open to disease, so I started to brush down the parts that felt open, and at the lectern I saw a woman crying. She was wearing a bonnet and a man came up to her holding a handkerchief and he was bald, but he'd combed his hair over, and then they disappeared.

I heard the doors go and the undertakers came through. Mr Sparrow said, – The next mourners need to prepare now, son.

They were walking up the aisle. I said, – I saw her at the lectern, and then I saw a woman and a man.

I didn't even believe it myself. But I knew I had seen all this with my own eyes.

Mr Sparrow said, after a second, – It's been a stressful day for you. I tell you, son, what will help is if you get a drink down you at the wake. Talk about her. Let other people tell you about her.

He moved his hand slowly and put it round my elbow.

– I'll show you what I mean, I said.

I went up to the lectern and tried to adjust it, but I didn't feel anything. It was just a lectern in a hall in front of your dead body.

Mr Sparrow said, – We have to be fair on the next mourners, sir.

I ignored him. I started moving the lectern around but nothing happened. I did some of my finger-strumming rituals that you used to find funny when we were kids, even though I didn't feel the need to do them. But nothing was happening.

I followed Mr Sparrow down the aisle and I heard a younger undertaker whisper, – What is it with this guy and funerals?

Mr Sparrow told him to be quiet.

I shook the hands of a hundred people, all offering

their condolences and offering to buy me a drink at the wake.

But I wasn't listening.

All I could think about was you.

6PM

At the Steamboat, Aunty kept on trying to get our little cousins to come over to me in the corner. But they could see that I didn't want to talk. I pretended to go to the toilet and left through the beer garden.

An envelope was half hanging out of our letterbox. I pushed it in with my knuckle, careful to only use the middle one so I didn't feel unclean.

A woman walked through our front door as if it wasn't there.

She was big, and her skin looked as if she had spent most of her life under the faraway sun and not the clouds of the dockland sky. She was wearing a blue apron and a scarf of yellow around her head, and she walked straight past me and she was gone.

I just wanted it to stop.

I wanted to feel clean again.

I let myself in. One of your boxes on the sofa had some papers peeping out the side. I had to sort them, to make sure they were all straight and in a line. I took them and jabbed them tidy on the floor, then stacked them back in the box.

And I saw you.

This time you were looking out the window. You were wearing that dark blue hoodie you never gave me back.

You shut the curtain and disappeared.

I nudged the box again, but it didn't work. It felt like it was where it was supposed to be. I tried once more but I knew I was wasting my time.

Then I heard the front door. I walked out of the living room and there was a man dressed in black stood by the stairs. I vaguely recalled him waiting in line to shake my hand, because he had a big collar.

I didn't want another person asking if they could do anything to help. So I said, – You know, it's rude to just walk into people's houses.

And he said, – Didn't you hear me calling?

– This is kind of a shit day for me.

– I didn't mean to barge in. I didn't know how else to get your attention, sorry. My name is Ted Hurley. Your sister was my doctoral student.

When you got accepted, I remember you telling me how excited you were by your new supervisor. He was why you chose your home town over Bristol in the first place.

I said, – Alexis told me about you. Didn't you go out of your way to help her get that bursary?

He said, – I guess so. Anyway, I'm sorry to bother you at this time. It's just that what I wanted to ask is better coming from me in person. I was wondering if you knew what she did with her thesis?

– Why do you need that? I said.

– She only uploaded certain chapters to her student records. But I know she was very close to submitting, and I feel that if I handed it in with a strong letter of recommendation, her doctorate could be awarded posthumously.

I couldn't explain how I regretted it now, how when we went to Aunty's birthday we ended up ignoring each other. So I said, – I don't know anything about it, to be honest. We fell out a few weeks ago.

Here is something I will never get the chance to say. Do you remember, when we last spoke, how you said I was smothering you after I accused you of being really distant lately? It wasn't you who was being the dickhead.

He said, after a moment or so, – Do you have any of her study stuff here? I mean I know it's not ideal, but if I could take it off you now I could submit it by the end of the academic year.

We went into the living room. I pointed at your boxes and turned to the window. I opened the curtains to give him more light, but I couldn't stop tugging the one on the left, even though it was fully back. And then I got the urge to stub my toe and out of nowhere I saw four men at a table playing cards.

Two of them were black and one white and one from the Middle East, but they didn't have any feet, their ankles in the ground. They were not quite there, as if I was looking at their reflections in a pane of glass. They were smoking and one of them laughed, and then they were gone.

I looked at Hurley. In the end, he said, – I'm not sure what I saw there.

– I'm more glad that it's not just in my head, I said.

Then he looked at me straight and said, – It's not just in your head. I don't know how else to say this, but you've worked out how to loop.

6.20PM

He said, – I can't explain what I mean without showing you.

So I said, – Then show me.

When I shut the front door, I squeezed the handle until my hand cramped. Now I could tell myself that the pain meant I didn't have to go back and check it was locked.

Hurley was waiting for me by the gate. – Took you a while to close the door, he said.

– I like to double check.

– You mean you had to perform a ritual.

He turned and walked. He would only know this if he did the same thing.

We went past a bunch of boys listening to some tinny grime on a phone, and made our way through the maze of the estate where the cars can't go.

Hurley said, – What do you know of the history of this place?

– Not as much as my sister.

We joined the road and got to Callaghan Square, the one with the tall glass banks and the fountain on the edge of town. He said, – OK then. Any idea what was here before this corporate monstrosity?

And I said, – This was all a building site when I was a kid.

– It was the Greek part of the city, he said. – Right next to the Somali quarter. Sailors brought their families over and settled in the streets where this square now is. They came from all over the world, and other sailors would meet Welsh women here and get married and make this their home port.

He looked around, then took off his shoe and lined it up so that it was perpendicular to the fountain.

I had felt the type of look on his face on my own. He had to get it right. It had to be perfect or it would leave him unclean. Then he took out some keys and arranged them until they were in a star shape and put them on the floor.

There were little kids playing in the fountain. Two brown boys wearing shorts and shoes and three white girls in long dresses. The girl in front turned around and she was smiling and running and then they were gone.

He put his shoe back on as I asked him what the fuck, but he walked off back towards the estate and I had to run to catch up. I asked him again, but there were some men waiting to be let inside the Salvation Army.

When I told him to slow down he stopped and picked up a couple of stones from the gutter. He put a few of them in a triangle and twisted his ear and I saw a bunch of black men in the road. One was rolling up a sleeve and two others were watching another man check how many bullets he had in a gun.

– I always feel bad for these guys, Hurley said. – A big crowd of demobbed Kiwi soldiers has barricaded them inside their lodgings. All for the crime of having jobs and being black.

And I said, – But that's not possible. That's the race riots of 1919.

He looked at me and said, – That's what it is, though. We're seeing ghosts. These are the animations of past lives. When people experience a moment of high emotion, like joy or love or stress, an imprint gets stored where it happened. Events of the past are all around us, and if you can bring about just the right conditions, they can be released for all the world to see.

I sat on the kerb. He sat down next to me and I said, – This is a lot to take in.

– It gets quite cool after a while, he said. – I've seen Henry VIII with half his nose lost to syphilis. I'm one of the few who've seen Caesar greeting Cleopatra for the first time at the gates of Rome.

I said, – One of the few?

– Let's just say we're not the only ones.

I thought about what it could mean. I didn't really care to see old kings and queens. If Hurley could see them, however, then maybe I could see Mum and you.

I said, – I think I wanna give it another try.

We walked back towards the dock, past the Lagos cafe and the turning for the mosque. Hurley stopped and said, – There's one here. You'll learn that. Look at that kerb jutting out.

It looked like any other. A car went past. I felt nothing.

He sighed and kicked a cigarette packet from the gutter and scratched his left knee.

Out of nowhere, a pretty young woman in a bonnet was looking at me. She was sat down at a table and she smiled. But this smile felt like it was for me. It was as if our eyes connected. The feeling of unease it gave me was enough to put a chill up my spine.

When she disappeared, I said, – I swear she could see me.

– Don't forget that it's an animation, Hurley said. – She's in a dockside cafe, trying to catch a sailor's eye so he would go in and give her business. She was rather famous, actually.

– What was her name?

– Mary Jane Kelly.

I shrugged and said nothing.

– Maybe you haven't heard of Mary Jane Kelly. But I bet you've heard of the man who killed her.

There was only one person he could mean. Everyone knew the stories. So I said, – I guess she must have been one of the Butcher of Butetown's victims.

– The Butcher never actually killed in Butetown, you know. He did them all in other parts of the city. That was just the racism of the time. People back then believed that the murders couldn't have been done by someone of good Welsh stock, they must have been done by a foreigner. Mary Jane Kelly, this poor young girl, maybe spooked by the reports of the Butcher in the papers, left for London. Then a couple of years later, on a wet, cold night in November 1888, this unlucky girl became the final known victim of Jack the Ripper.

I said nothing.

– Now you try, he said.

I smoothed down my arms. I picked up the cigarette packet and dropped it on its side. And then you appeared in front of us. You were hopping on one foot and bending down and then you disappeared.

For a long moment, we were silent. And then Hurley said, – I wish she'd told me.

6.50PM

You never had to step in and out of rooms on the same foot like I have to and you never touched the fridge door with every finger before you opened it. Mum always joked that you were the normal one. You were the studious one who followed after her, and I was the scatterbrain who was like the dad we had never known.

– What do you mean? I said to Hurley. – Alexis could do this too?

– She kept on doing the same thing, he said. – It doesn't really work that way. Maybe she was teaching herself.

I looked at the time on my phone. I had been gone nearly an hour. I walked off and said, – Come and talk it over at the Steamboat. People will start noticing I'm not there.

He caught up and we walked past the train station but he didn't answer, as if he was stopping himself from saying something.

Then he said, – It would only take five minutes to check all those boxes for her thesis. I know what I'm looking for.

But I had already seen enough of you today. So I said, – Give me your address and I'll post it.

He stopped walking and said, – I'll still have to make a case for it, you know. And the thesis itself could be worth something. It's one of the most important the history department has ever seen. I could help turn it in to a popular history book. It's ostensibly about the lives of the nine individuals the Butcher of Butetown killed, and she made a compelling case for a few more victims that have never been considered in the modern field of Butcherology. But she also told me at our last meeting that while this wasn't what the thesis was about, she actually got right to the heart of the identity of the Butcher himself.

I had no answer. Deep down I knew that going to the wake was not about saying goodbye. It was about having so many drinks that I would be too drunk to think. Yet here someone stood, giving me a proper chance to do one last thing for you.

And, to be brutally honest, I could do with the money. We never came from a rich family. When Mum wasn't working, she gave most of her time away to those boring council meetings she used to obsess over. It had been five years. The payout from her death had almost gone.

I could see the Steamboat up ahead on the corner. Someone from the wake was outside, in all black, puffing out a big cloud of vape smoke. But instead of going back, we turned right at the junction and headed towards the estate. Hurley looked nervous as we passed some of the boys, but they knew why we were wearing black and they got out of our way.

Back in the house again, he looked through the four boxes on the sofa while I started on the eight stacked in the corner.

– Are you sure this is everything? he soon said. – It's unusual for a PhD student not to have reams and reams of notes.

– I wish I knew what to say, I said.

He sat down on the sofa between two boxes. He scratched his head. Then he said, – Are you sure she wasn't here recently? There's something about the cut of the carpet. I don't know. It just feels like an emotionally charged space.

I knew the truth. If it was emotionally charged it's cos I had been a bit of a prat to you. But instead we stacked the boxes against the far wall. Hurley stared at the space, hand on chin, and looked around. He moved the sofa an inch or two back and tilted the rug. Then he walked through to the kitchen and came back with a tin of tomatoes. He put it down next to the boxes.

A man in his fifties, eyes sharp as a twist of lemon, was walking towards us. He had a small boat on his back, almost like a shell. On each side of his neck from a rope hung a large salmon. He walked knee deep through the room and he was gone.

I knew why you didn't appear. The can was the wrong way round for a start, and the rug needed to be symmetrical with the edge of the wall. It was driving me nuts just looking at them.

Before Hurley said anything, I straightened the carpet and turned the can.

I stepped back and you were there, in your denim jacket and black tee like the last time we saw each other. You looked around and grabbed a pile of papers from the sofa, then chucked them in your satchel and ran for the kitchen.

– Did you see those papers? Hurley said. – That could have been her thesis.

I weighed my words before I spoke. I said, – In the middle of the page it said Festival of the Ghost.

Hurley clenched a fist and said, – I knew it. That was the title. Her research was tied into a religious holiday.

– She was wearing those same clothes the last time I saw her, I said. – I've thought about that night more than any other of my life.

Hurley stayed silent. – Your connection with her is obviously a lot stronger than mine, he said after a while. – You could probably trace her steps and find her thesis quite quickly. I can help if you feel like giving it a go.

I said yes, and we walked back to the Steamboat. We shook hands outside as Hurley insisted that he had an early start. I went back in. Everyone was at the merry stage of reminiscence, but looking for your thesis was all I could think about. Because while I had told Hurley the title, what I didn't tell him was what was scribbled in pencil underneath: a single line of three words, saying, KEEP SAFE DANGER.

1 APRIL

12PM

You would have been proud. My post-wake hangover lasted three days, and it was another two before my energy was near its pre-wake level. When the withdrawal anxiety finally dissipated I sent Hurley an email.

I walked the two miles to his part of the city. He lived in one of the few townhouses on the leafy terrace not converted to luxury apartments or offices. I rang the bell under the keypad and he opened the door and said, – I'll just get my coat.

I asked to use the bathroom and he let me up the stairs. I walked into an en suite bedroom, and after using it I couldn't help but have a quick peek out on the balcony. I opened up the doors, and I was overlooking a long, wooden-decked garden full of potted bushes. But the balcony itself just wasn't right. So I went over to a plant in the corner and positioned the pot so it was equidistant from the wall, and then I pulled the glass table over slightly so the legs weren't on the cracks between the slats, and out of nowhere I saw Hurley dressed in white, eyes closed, kneeling in front of me. Next to him was a blonde woman, maybe a few years younger.

I heard the doors to the balcony open, and the woman I had just seen kneeling was stood there.

– Don't you know it's rude to spy? she said. I said, – I didn't mean to.

Hurley walked out. I knew it was the real Hurley and not the loop I had just seen because he wasn't wearing white. The woman shot him a look so dirty I thought she was about to butt him. She walked back inside without saying a word.

– I'm so sorry, I said. – I didn't know that would happen.

– You'll learn to control it soon.

I said, – I'll be more careful.

– Don't worry. It was just a private moment. We're Church in Wales, you see. You know the big church in the middle of town, St Dyfrig's? That's where we worship. It has the most beautiful organ, almost all walnut and gold. I've been helping to restore the old bugger these past few months.

– I'll go apologise.

Hurley shook his head. – She's just worried that the neighbours might get confused if they see us disappear. I once rearranged our furniture on the top floor and the couple next door saw an old footman in a tin bath. You could hear their screams through the wall.

He turned to leave, but then he said, – Hey, you want to see something cool?

He led me into the bedroom. He made me help him shove the wrought iron bed into the corner, and he got some coins out of his pocket and stacked them on top of each other. Then he rotated them slightly and stepped back and we saw a man in a white shirt with a black neckerchief working at a Singer sewing machine. He had a short moustache and was sweating. But that's not what drew me. He had a look of absolute rage on his face, as if he hated the fact that he had to sew. He wanted to tear the fabric in half with his teeth. Then he stopped sewing and looked straight ahead. He was breathing deeply and then he was gone.

I was about to say something – that out of all the people I had seen, this man had spooked me the most, when Hurley raised a finger and rotated the coins the other way. Then, sat in almost the exact same spot was a brown man in a T-shirt, making a checked shirt against another sewing machine. He was talking to someone and then he smiled as he wiped his brow and disappeared.

– That first man, Hurley said, – Was a farmboy from the Gwent Levels who came to the city for work in the 1880s. The second man was a Bengali who escaped the civil war and worked here in the 1970s. Sat in the same place, doing the same work, ninety years apart. Some things never change.

We moved the bed back and Hurley said he was off to calm down his girlfriend. I shut the door to the balcony. The bed was at the wrong angle now, and so were the curtains, but I was scared to touch them in case I looped Hurley and his girlfriend again. I stayed there till I heard their voices calm down then went to wait outside.

12.30PM

When Hurley eventually joined me, I noticed that he had a nick on his cheekbone. He didn't look me in the eye and he told me not to ask. I took him down a long terrace adjacent to his own but the other side of the main road and I said, – This is the one. I remember the day I helped her move in.

Your fuchsias were still outside, potted and purple

and pink. I knocked but no answer came. I tried again and nothing.

– No answer, no worry, Hurley said. – People are predictable.

He put his arm out and motioned for me to stand back. He scratched behind his ear and pulled a hair out of his head and stroked the floor with it. Then he stepped back himself, and out of nowhere came a woman in a green and pink sari, leading a small child inside by the hand.

– Maybe I got the wrong house, I said. – But I remember the fuchsias.

– Early eighties, I would imagine, Hurley said after a second. – Maybe that small kid now owns this place and rents it out. You give it a try.

I rotated the fuchsias and straightened the leaves. You came out of the door. You were stood in front of us, wearing your coat with the furry collar. You looked around, put a key where the plant pot was, and moved it back into place.

– Should have checked there first, Hurley said.

He picked up the pot, and sure enough, underneath it in the soil was a single brass key. He put it in the door and turned.

We were in the short dark hallway. I couldn't

hear a thing, so I walked to your room and opened it, empty as when I'd left it two weeks ago.

– This is Alexis' old room, I said, quietly. – Nothing here.

Hurley walked in and looked around. He opened the door to the walk-in wardrobe and saw nothing. – I can't feel anything, Hurley said. – You?

I shook my head.

Hurley walked out into the corridor. He went up the stairs.

– What are you doing? I said. But he held a finger to his lips. He popped his head into the bathroom, then turned around to go into another room.

I followed after him. He was in was your old housemate's room. I had only met her twice. The day you moved in and the day of your funeral. Once in hope and once in despair.

I said, – I'm not sure I'm comfortable with this.

– We've already broken in.

I had no answer. I watched Hurley look through the drawers and check out the bookcase. Then he looked in the wardrobe, shut the doors, turned to face me and I shrugged.

We went back down the stairs and into the kitchen. There was just enough space in the middle for us to fit without touching shoulders. I took a plate from the draining board and positioned it on the counter. Then I tapped the plate in the centre three times and stepped back myself, and I saw you again, arms crossed, leaning against the side.

In front of you stood a woman I had never seen before. She was wearing a green turtleneck and was perhaps the same age as Hurley. Her hair was of henna and cut into a bob. She was talking as much with her hands as with her face.

Then you uncrossed your arms, reached behind and grabbed a load of paper. You tried to hand it to the woman, but she stepped back as if she didn't want to take it. You kept arguing and then you both went.

– That didn't look good, I said.

– I will have to concur.

– Who was that?

Hurley said nothing, looking at the counter. Then he said, – Professor Jayne Mimpriss.

His face gave nothing away. I was just about to ask when he said, – She's a colleague. A real difficult one.

– Why would she be here?

– I wasn't your sister's only PhD Supervisor. I was Alexis' primary and Mimpriss was her secondary.

I crossed my arms, and realised I was leaning on the counter in the same way you did. Then I said, – Can't you speak to her?

– Let's just say that we don't get along. She's the departmental dragon, if you get what I mean.

– I'll talk to her then.

– I wouldn't recommend it.

– Someone has to.

Hurley sighed, and said, – Just be careful with how much information you share with her. Ask straight questions, and if you don't get a straight answer, leave.

We walked out the kitchen and into the noise of the street.

1 PM

After a ten-minute shortcut past an outdoor market on a street full of mobile repair shops, we were on the new campus in Cathays. We got to one of the newer buildings, all silver and chrome, which had small porthole windows and a tiered roof. Hurley led me through the front and he nodded at the big security guard behind the desk. When we got out of the lift he led me past his own office and pointed to another a few doors down.

– Probably best you don't mention me, he said. – And good luck.

I put my ear to the door and heard low voices. A

note on the door beneath a history cafe leaflet stated that today was Mimpriss' office hours. The next slot was clear. I wouldn't need that much time.

I waited five minutes and a student, wearing a long scarf wrapped many times around her neck, opened the door and walked past me. I let it shut, gave it another minute, and knocked.

The same woman I saw in your old house was sat typing. I recognised the nose, the short daintiness of it, and the choppy henna hair.

– Professor Mimpriss? I said. – I'm Alexis' brother, Levi.

She paused. – Oh, right, she said, and looked down and shook her head slightly. – Of course. Please come in.

I sat down.

– Sorry to drop in on you like this.

– I'm sorry I didn't make the funeral, she said. – I hope she had a good send-off.

– She did. But I'm not here to talk about that.

Mimpriss shifted back in her seat. – Go on.

– I'm actually here to ask you about Alexis' thesis.

Mimpriss stayed silent. Then she looked down and said, – I'm afraid I don't have it. She uploaded a few chapters to the university portal, but she opted to submit everything as a hard copy.

– That's a pity, I said. – She tried to give it to you, didn't she? A couple of weeks ago.

Her hand came up to her necklace. She started idly playing with the cross hanging from it as she said, – How do you know that?

– She mentioned something, I said, trying my luck. – She said you had some sort of argument.

– Did she say what about?

– I was hoping you could tell me.

She said, – It was nothing. We were arguing about a woman called Mari McBryde.

– Someone you knew?

Mimpriss leaned back in her chair and stopped playing with the cross.

– Mari was a destitute woman who lived around here in the 1880s. She was stabbed thirty-nine times on the stairway to a row of flats. Alexis was convinced she was murdered by the unidentified man the newspapers named the Butcher of Butetown, and I was telling her it was probably two drunk privates from the Glamorganshire Dragoons. But she was having none of it.

– I see, I said, and saw that Mimpriss' hand had again come back to the cross.

– I wish I could help you further, she said. – If you come across it, please let me know. I would like to see if I could get her PhD awarded posthumously. You'll have to excuse me now, as this is my office hours day.

She took her hand away from the cross and started clicking on a mouse.

I got up to leave but said, – Are you religious, Dr Mimpriss?

She didn't turn to look at me. – Yes, she said. – Church in Wales.

A popular one in this department, I thought. I was going to mention Hurley, but then I remembered his words about bringing up his name. So I said, – I hear St Dyfrig's has the most beautiful organ.

– A highlight of every service.

I knew that organ was being fixed. I stopped my eyes from pursing and said, – Still works fine after all these years?

Mimpriss sighed and said, – Never worked better.

I thought of the pencil note on the front of your thesis.

– Can I ask you one more question? I said, and her loud clicking made me feel like it wouldn't be a welcome one. – Can I just ask what you know about the Festival of the Ghost?

She grabbed the cross with both hands and turned to look at me.

– How about I ask you what you know about it, Levi? she said.

– I know Alexis' thesis had something to do with it, I said.

Mimpriss stayed still. She stared at me and even though I felt uncomfortable, I stared back.

Then she said, – You shouldn't ask about that. If I were you, I would pretend I had never heard of it. The church that celebrates it is very powerful, and you wouldn't want them to know that you know anything about them.

She carried on staring at me until I left the room.

I got my phone out and searched for the Festival of the Ghost. Nothing came up. I changed the search engine but still got nothing, so I walked down the corridor and knocked on Hurley's door.

1.15PM

Hurley was on the phone. He raised a hand and said his goodbyes. I walked into the room proper and he said, – Did you get anywhere?

I shook my head. – You were right about her being difficult.

– What happened?

– I think she threatened me.

Hurley raised his eyebrows and said, – Maybe I should raise that with the head of department.

– I don't want any trouble. She told me she was a member of St Dyfrig's Church. You remember what you told me, about the organ? She said it works fine.

Hurley scowled and said, – I was literally cleaning the pipe divisions on Monday. Even if we went to different services she would know this.

– I was thinking similar. But then I mentioned the Festival of the Ghost to her.

– You didn't.

– Couldn't help myself. The more I know, the better my chances of finding the thesis. Then she told me to stay away, and to forget that I'd ever heard of anything.

Hurley looked down at his desk. Then he said, – Most of what I know about it came from your sister. It's one of the main religious holidays of a small sect known as the Spiritists. Their main church is not far from here, as it happens. The Spirit Freedom Centre.

– It rings a vague bell. Maybe I should check it out. You never know, I might get a loop of her.

– I would have to advise against it. She never had anything good to say about them.

– I can look after myself.

He was playing at the nick that his girlfriend had

given him. Probably to try and avoid rolling his eyes. Then he said, – I've got a few things to do this afternoon, but I'll give you a call and we could go down together.

He picked the phone up again. I excused myself from his office and headed to the lift. I knew what I needed to do. While I appreciated his sentiment, I didn't need a chaperone.

1.30PM

A couple of minutes later and I had reached a street where my phone told me the Spirit Freedom Centre stood, and I found myself walking down a tall Victorian terrace with small tiled gardens full of plant pots, under a canopy of fresh blossom and bright green leaves. But halfway down, the houses abruptly stopped. A low-lying newbuild block of brown-bricked flats stood right at the pavement edge, followed by a brutal, tiered brown square of a building. The top tier was a huge glass dome. Luftwaffe clearance, no doubt, a common sight the closer you got to the docks. I approached tiered building, not taking my eyes off it for a second.

It was an awful looking church. And it seemed so out of place, tucked away down a side street. No wonder, according to the article I read, it had taken so long to get planning permission.

I didn't feel anything on the outside. I peeked my head in and saw an empty reception desk. Ahead there was another door, slightly ajar. I went in, pushing what Mimpriss had said to the back of my mind.

The pews on all four sides faced a large black altar in the middle. The light from the dome filled the room and made it glow. I walked through the pews till I was underneath. I could feel that something wasn't right straight away. I brushed my fingers across the altar as if I were sweeping dust and tapped it twice. Then a suited, clean-shaven man appeared in front of me. On his raised hand he had a tattoo. It looked like three lines of Latin, but I couldn't work out what it said. Then he was gone.

I wondered if getting a tattoo on the palm was more painful than getting one on a more traditional part of the body like the shoulder, but I heard a noise and when I turned round, a blonde woman in a blue blouse walked in.

She said, – Excuse me, but you're not supposed to be in here.

I said, – I'm very sorry. I assumed the church was open. I just wanted to pray. She smiled and said, – I don't think I've ever seen you at a service before.

– I'm new around here, I said, and I started to walk through the pews back towards the entrance.

– Membership of this church is by invitation only.

– That's OK. I was curious about this place because I had heard about the Festival of the Ghost. Do you have any leaflets about it?

The polite face she had been wearing disappeared. She said, – Why don't you tell me what you know first?

But before I could think of anything to say she said, – Stay here. I'll fetch someone to talk to you.

She left, but it felt like all the good energy was leaking out of the small gap where the door didn't completely shut behind her. So I closed it slowly, and gave in to the urge to press down on a tile with my foot.

The man with the Latin tattoo came back: he was walking towards the door. He was rubbing something in a cloth. Before he disappeared, I saw that it was a knife.

I heard more footsteps. The woman came back in the room. Behind her was a big guy a couple of years older than me in a boxy grey suit. His neck looked like it could pull a lorry.

He said, – So you're the young man who's asking about the festival. I nodded and said, – It was just a general enquiry.

– Why don't we start by you telling us what you know about it?

He was trying to stare through me. I figured I had nothing to lose from the truth, so I said, – My sister was writing her thesis on it before she died. I was just thinking that any information might lead me to find it so I can get her PhD awarded.

The man said, – Follow me.

1.40PM

He led me to a door the other side of the altar and ushered me to go in first. I walked down a corridor, aware he was staying close. We passed three doors and a fire exit and went up a flight of stairs. At the top was a small hallway. When the man knocked at the door, I saw that he had a tattoo on his palm also.

Another big man watched me walk in, one hand clasped onto the opposite wrist. Behind a large ebony desk sat the man I had looped.

I felt all the eyes on me. The man behind the desk said, – Please, have a seat.

I walked forward and sat down. The man who had led me up the stairs came and stood to the left of the desk.

– Mr Coburn, the man at the desk said. – Some water.

The minder-type bloke went to a side cabinet, and the man at the desk said, – I see you have already met my colleague, Mr Radar. My other friend is Mr Coburn. I am Mr Turner.

When he offered me his hand, I found myself looking for the tattoo I had seen on his palm, and he caught me. The man called Coburn brought over two glasses of water and put them on the table. I took a sip of mine, and as I put it down, Turner looked at it then leaned over and moved my glass back a half-inch.

It was a tell-tale sign. It was exactly the kind of thing I do. The glass had to be perfect on the table or it would drive him nuts.

Turner took a sip from his own drink, and he put it down and started rotating the glass. He was watching me as he did this, and I could tell he was trying to find the precise location that would make him feel comfortable. He said, as he was doing this, – So I hear you're interested in a certain festival.

I said, – Only in a nominal way. I'm trying to find my sister's thesis. She was writing about it, I believe.

– I'm sorry, Turner said. – But I have no idea what you're talking about.

– My sister or the festival?

– Both.

– I doubt you knew her. She passed away recently.

He sat back in his chair. – I'm sorry for your loss, he said. – But she will always be there in a way. One of our fundamental teachings is that the past is with us in the present.

I nodded. He stayed silent. I could see that it was pointless being here. I got up from my chair and turned to leave and offered a hand and thanked him for his time. I looked down for the tattoo on his palm.

We met eyes, and I could tell that he caught me looking again.

– I always wanted to get a tattoo but never got round to it, I said. – They seem to be pretty popular with members of this church.

He paused. – Not members, per se. Just those who work for the church.

– Do you all have the same Latin or is it just you?

He looked over my shoulder briefly then said, – When did you see me with Latin?

– I must have got it wrong, I said. – It looked like Latin.

Turner stared at me. He didn't offer to show me his palm.

I nodded and said I would see myself out. He told me to stop but I closed the door, walked across the foyer and ran down the stairs. At the bottom, I looked round and saw the two other men following quickly. I went round the corridor, saw the doors in a row and ran to the fire exit, coming through the back near some train arches. I turned right and walked as fast as I could down the street. I passed a woman on a phone pushing a pram, and wondered if the men would try anything in such a busy place.

I was thankful for the busyness of the city for once, thankful that there were hundreds of eyes and feet and that nothing could happen without a hundred witnesses. I crossed over between the traffic, narrowly avoiding a man on a scooter who beeped. I ran into the market. I crouched between a florist and a butchers and saw the two men enter. I watched them discuss something for a second and Coburn walked straight ahead while Radar turned left. As soon as they were both out of eyesight, I walked quickly back the way I came, passed an old church and headed into a pub called the Glendower.

2.30PM

I was on my second pint when Hurley walked in. He declined my offer to get him one. I explained my visit to the Spirit Freedom Centre in as much detail as I could remember, and about the loop of the man with the palm tattoo holding a knife. He listened without interjecting. When I got to the bit about escaping and running into the pub, he shook his head and said, – They know you're here.

– I managed to lose them.

Hurley lent his elbow on the table and leaned in close and said, – You can't protect yourself from these people. They will be gathering information on you even now. They'll know about me and you and where you live by the end of the day. Within the week, they'll know more about you and your habits and actions than even Facebook and Google.

He went to the bar and came back with two double whiskies. We offered a salute to you and I was grateful for the warmth of the drink, that it made me feel something that wasn't sorrow or anxiety.

Then Hurley, after wiping his mouth on his sleeve, said, – The people you saw at the church: most of them are like me and you. They can loop, and they're very good at it. They are generally very rich and have huge resources of people around them. You would be amazed by how far people will go to get them what they want. They can blackmail people so easily, because most of your deeds involving emotion are recorded. Imagine knowing the password to every account owned by a pop star. Imagine knowing that the CEO of a company likes getting his nipples clamped while dressed as a baby. They know everything. They've probably gone back to where they last saw you and as soon as they were confident no one was looking, they've looped your last movements.

– I wish I had another double in front of me.

– Are you sure it was just the two of them?

I nodded. – Two big guys who looked like they didn't belong in suits. One was called Coburn and the other Radar.

Hurley shook his head. He went into his laptop bag and pulled out a green hooded top.

He said, – They're probably on each door. This is my workout hoodie. Sorry if it stinks. Put it on, and when everyone leaves, put the hood up and meet me next to the antique map stall in the market.

I was about to ask why everyone would leave, but Hurley got up and headed for the gents. I put the hoody on. It barely fitted over my shoulders. But then the fire alarm went off, and I saw the two barmen look at each other as everyone in the bar stopped talking.

Most people left through the front door, but I put my hood up and kept my head down as I walked out of the fire exit next to the toilet.

There were close to a hundred people out on the pavement, adding to the traffic of passers-by and the smokers already in the chalked-out area. I found myself almost pinned against the boarded up window of an old bookmakers next to the pub, between a single white flower stuck to the wall and the masses of people who had left at the same time. I couldn't see Coburn and Radar, so I kept my head down and walked away.

I turned back to look eventually, as I got to the market. They were both high up on the steps of St Dyfrig's Church, watching everyone walking past, looking out for me and me alone.

2.45PM

The market was full. I walked around the stalls, still with my hood up, as the stallholders eyed me. At last in the fourth row, between a candlemaker and a stall selling houseplants, I spotted Hurley looking at an antique map of Byzantium.

He put it down and said, – They see you?

– They're still looking from the stairs of the church.

– Good. That should give us some time.

He led me through the stalls selling Welsh cakes and scarves and we left through a side entrance. The streets became quieter the further we got from the market, but the buildings got bigger and the glass more reflective. Then we rounded another corner, went through a passage and came through into the small quiet calm of Shields square. A couple of builders in high vis were eating some sandwiches on a silver bench that cut through the middle.

Hurley watched them, sat down on a different bench and said, – We'll have to wait until those workmen leave.

– How come?

– Doesn't matter. For now, let me tell you about the Spiritists. I've been researching them ever since I discovered I had these abilities when I was a teenager.

I watched the builders laugh at something that the younger one was showing them on his phone. Then I said, – Why didn't you mention anything before?

– Because I didn't have to.

The builders got up and started walking towards one of the other passages that led into the square.

– The man you saw with the tattoo, Hurley said. – His name is Peter Blake Turner. His father, the man who set up the church in the sixties, was called Frederick James Turner. The younger Turner likes to model himself on his old man.

Hurley looked around, and he motioned for me

to get up. We went over to some iron railings in the corner. Hurley looked again, and saw that we were all alone.

He said, – The Spiritists believe that by keeping the images of those no longer alive, and honouring them, they are doing God's work. But as it's normally our memories of high emotion that are preserved, it means that a high number of murders are stored. By re-enacting them, they believe that the memory, that is the original, may have more energy to flourish.

He looked around once more, then shut his eyes. A second or two more and he swept the floor with his hands and spat.

Turner was there again, albeit looking older. He had his hands around an old man's neck. The old man was trying to stop him, but then other sets of hands came and held him down.

I could see the old man choking, the anguish on his face. My heart beat like a drum. But Turner got a knife, and he slit at the old man's throat. The blood spurted to the floor.

I wanted it to stop. I had never seen anything so disgusting in my life.

Turner went to the old man's face, and nicked off the end of his nose. He carved a ^ underneath each eye, and I thought I would puke in the street.

I braced my arms on my knees like I'd just run a race.

– That was Turner senior, re-enacting an earlier murder by the Butcher of Butetown, on its one hundredth anniversary. I have no idea who the man was. Probably no one that anyone would notice when he went missing.

– Why the fuck did you show me that?

– So you know what they do.

– I think I'm gonna be sick.

Hurley laughed and said, – He didn't even do that one right.

I walked over to one of the benches. Shields Square didn't feel as calm any more. I said, – I've heard enough.

Hurley sat down next to me. – I'm sorry, he said. – I guess you get used to seeing things like that after a while.

I said nothing. I wanted nothing more at that moment to do with loops, or the Spiritists or Hurley. I never wanted to see another ghost ever again.

I said, – Just as well it's a dead end with those sickos on the thesis anyway.

– Why don't we try back at the flat again?

– There wasn't anything there.

Hurley looked straight ahead. – Well, where else could Alexis have been?

I thought for a second. No clues from Hurley, no clues from the Spirit Freedom Centre. I thought back earlier in the day.

– Professor Mimpriss said they were arguing about Mari McBryde, whoever that is.

Hurley stood up and said, – Let's give her a visit.

3.30PM

After a few minutes, Hurley stopped and pointed to a small, arched passage between two houses. We walked under and saw a group of maybe twenty people ahead of us in a circle.

A woman in a yellow coat in the centre was talking. It took me a second to realise where I knew her from.

– Looks like a tour, Hurley said. – The Butcher of Butetown is big business around here.

– She was at the funeral, I said. – The one in the yellow coat doing all the talking.

Hurley looked over. He said, – Did Alexis ever mention anyone like her?

– Don't think so.

Hurley motioned for me to follow him back down

the passage. When we got back to the street, he said, – This can't be a coincidence.

– What do you mean?

– She's not hosting a tour over there.

– Then what is she doing?

– I think that's a Spiritist meeting. If I'm not mistaken, it's not long until the Festival of the Ghost.

I looked over at the crowd. It was a good mix of ages. Some were carrying cameras around their necks. I said, – They look like a bunch of tourists.

He said, – You're not giving them enough credit.

Hurley watched the crowd and played with the nick on his cheek. After two minutes, the woman led them down the other end of the alley and they rounded a corner.

We walked to where they had been. The buildings either side of us were fairly new. They hadn't had time for the bricks to chip even, or for people to hang blinds at wonky angles.

Hurley pointed above us and said, – There used to be an old, damp set of tenements where we're standing. The homeless used to sleep in the stairwell. A porter found Mari here one Tuesday morning in 1882.

I said, – I can't feel anything.

Hurley said, – I'll see what I can do.

He took a bottle out of his laptop case and placed

it on the edge of the kerb, and turned it so the label was facing one of the newbuilds. He stepped back and said, – You might not like what you're about to see.

A small woman was lying down, wearing a long skirt, but she was four feet above our heads. A man was over her. She was trying to wrestle his hands off her neck.

I said, – You said you wouldn't show me any more.

– Oh, This is one of the tame ones, Hurley said, not taking his eyes off.

The lapels were up on the man's long coat so I couldn't catch all of his face, but I could feel the anger in him from just the side of his temple. He let go with his right hand and went into his pocket and he was holding a knife. He stabbed the woman and I saw her body judder as he drew out the blade. Then he stabbed her again and again.

– Make it stop, I said.

– She's not real, Hurley said. – It's just an animation. Look at him stab. God, The Butcher had a bit of energy. Five, six, seven. You've got to toughen up if you're going to get used to looping. Eight, nine, ten.

The woman had stopped moving. But the man was on top of her, stabbing and stabbing and I just wanted him to stop.

I said, – There must be a way of ending it. Hurley

sighed. – I don't know why you care so much. Fourteen, fifteen, sixteen.

More blood came out of her with each stab. I had to make it stop. I took a step forward and I jumped to the woman and I tried to grab her, and I felt almost as if I was holding something, and I held strong and as my feet touched the ground I felt her come with me, and when I landed she was stood by my side, looking up. Then she looked me in the face. And she turned and walked and she was gone.

I felt a blow on my shoulder. – What the fuck did you just do? Hurley said.

– I don't fucking know, I said.

– Now we'll never know if she was the Butcher's first victim or not.

– I don't care.

We both noticed two figures walking towards us. I was looking at myself, beside Hurley. The other me and the other Hurley walked and stopped and looked up at the point where Mari had been murdered, and then they disappeared.

Hurley said, – Oh, God, look, they're all turning up. I told you it wasn't a coincidence.

He put his head down and marched away.

I saw two figures under the arch, and realised it was Coburn and Radar. I put my hood back up and walked off. When I got to the end of the alley I saw them stop where we had seen the murder. Coburn pinched some grit and threw it away.

Above him I saw the man strangling someone who was no longer there. They looked down the alley at me, and they started running.

3.45PM

Maybe if there were three of me we could collectively take on Coburn and Radar. But if there was only one of me then I would need five of Hurley.

I followed him down the cobbled alley and under another arch. The street we entered was busy with cars. I hurried ahead and darted between two vans.

– You can't hide, Hurley said as he passed. – Keep moving. Jump on a bus or a train if you can.

I could see Coburn and Radar making their way between the shoppers and pushchairs. I hurried on and caught up. The buildings went higher and the street narrower and with it the sky darker. I looked again and the men were close.

We neared a mini market on a corner. Hurley managed to cross the road before a van turned, but I had to stop before I got run down, and when it passed I couldn't see him anywhere.

I looked back and saw Coburn and Radar not thirty feet away. The street the van went down was Hurley's own, and I thought of course, he knows this area like the back of his hand.

I hadn't felt this alone since the first lockdown. But I had no time to think, no time to do anything but move. I went up the street past a blue gated school and the road jinked to the left, giving me a brief blind spot back towards where Coburn and Radar were. After the school was an alley, and I looked down it full of graff and behind the buildings I could see a yard, and maybe even another alley going off to the right.

I ran into the yard, but when I went to turn the corner expecting to see a way out I found myself faced with a barrier to a multistorey car park. I hurried into it before they spotted me, the warm air inside making me feel sick. It had a glass front, and I saw another exit next to a ticket machine.

I went towards it, but stopped. On the other side of the glass was the familiar yellow coat of the woman, speaking to the same enraptured crowd as earlier. If Hurley was right then I would have twenty Spiritists after me and not two. I went to turn around but I saw a loop of myself, and I heard Radar say, – He's in here somewhere.

I hid behind one of the pillars. I prayed that the woman in the yellow coat didn't turn around.

I could hear them muttering, discussing something. I knew I had maybe one chance to bolt out the way I came. Neither Coburn nor Radar looked like they could do parkour. And maybe I could use the cars to my advantage, hiding behind them. But then I saw a black rope come from my right, and before I could move I saw that it was a belt, it tightened and my head smacked against the pillar, and I got a black spot in my vision. I tried to move but I was jammed.

Coburn came from my right, and before I could even think to twist, he shovel-hooked a fist in my ribs and I couldn't breathe, the pain was too much.

He said, as I tried to get some air into my lungs, So what happened to Mari?

I tried to breathe using my stomach. When the next punch came, this time flat into my gut, I felt it on the inside of my spine. My legs went and I was held up purely by the belt around my neck, stopping me from getting any more of the air I so desperately needed.

Coburn pushed his face close. I wished I had the energy to grab at his ears or claw his eyes, but I was done.

He said, – Why isn't Mari McBryde getting stabbed no more? Was that you?

And the belt went slack and Coburn swung, but there was nothing I could do, and I felt the connect and the last thing I saw before everything went black was the side of Coburn's boot.

4PM

I heard footsteps and murmurs. I stayed tight in a ball so I could breathe.

I heard a woman say, – In 1882, this would have been the back garden of number 31. It was here that the unidentified murderer struck for the second time.

Then I heard another voice – deep and male – say, – Are you going to go through the whole tour calling him the unidentified murderer? Just say the Butcher of Butetown.

And I heard the woman say, – This is literally the spot where a boy had his eyes gouged out. If you wanted to think of the unidentified murderer as a loveable outlaw like Jack the Ripper then you're on the wrong tour.

There was silence, and even through my pain I felt uneasy. And then I heard another woman say, – What's that on the floor?

There were footsteps all around me. I opened my eyes.

The woman in the yellow coat bent down. – Are you OK? she said.

What Hurley had said kept coming back into my mind.

She put her hand on my knee. Someone tried to put a scarf under my head but I held a hand up to stop them.

I said that I didn't need help, but I couldn't turn to face the other way.

– I'll call an ambulance, a man said.

– Leave me, please, I said. – I don't need any help.

I pushed myself so I was sat up. It was difficult to find a comfortable spot on the pillar that didn't hurt my chest.

The woman in the yellow coat put her hand on my knee again. – It's Levi, isn't it? she said. – My name is Emily. I knew your sister. I used to help her with her research.

I said, – Just leave me alone.

Emily looked at the people around her. – OK, I was just saying, you look in bad shape.

I got to my feet, careful not to stand too straight so I could breathe. And I said, – I don't need your help.

– Alexis said you could be a dick sometimes but I was only trying to be nice.

I turned and limped through the car park as the crowd murmured, and the last thing I heard before walking back into the yard was Emily's voice go into Formal Mode as she started up once more.

4.30PM

I wiped my nose and felt the sting of it as I looked at the red on my cuff. There was no answer on Hurley's phone. Second knock on his door and he pulled me in.

– It's a little more than that nick on your cheek, I said.

He sat me in a wicker chair and said, – You should have gone straight to the hospital.

– I'm more concerned about going to a police station.

– You'd be better off laying low.

I didn't have the energy to argue. I undid my collar and lifted my shirt. The colour purple flashed back at me. He went off and came back with a hot flannel and a bowl full of warm water. I tapped the flannel on my nose. Still red.

– I need to know, I said. – If they could do this

then I need to know if they had anything to do with Alexis' death.

– We can always check, Hurley said. – It didn't happen far from here.

– Fuck no, I said.

– Sorry, terrible idea.

I felt around my ribs for signs of a break. After a while I said, – I saw the rest of them after. The group we saw before.

– I told you. We see them, and five minutes later those thugs are after us. It must have been a meet.

I didn't answer. I couldn't be so sure. I washed myself down but Hurley insisted on driving me to hospital. Then, when we got to the door, his phone started vibrating. He looked at the number, sighed, and said he had to take it.

He answered but didn't say anything. I gave him the thumbs up and let myself out as he turned and whispered into his phone.

It was going to be a long, painful walk. A two hour wait for an X-ray.

I went on your Facebook profile and searched your friends list for an Emily but nothing came up. I stood still for a second, then made up my mind and limped up the street. Five minutes later and I was at your old front door.

A light was on. I was about to knock, when instead I felt the urge to scrape my foot on the floor and polish the number. I stepped out of the space and I saw you, laughing, and going inside. And there, laughing behind you, I saw Emily.

8 APRIL

3PM

The only pleasure I could find through the pain was that it allowed me to avoid the boxes full of your stuff. The week lying in bed had given me plenty of time to think, and I now knew what I needed to do.

I was wearing Hurley's hoodie and the same jeans, so if Coburn or Radar looped me they wouldn't be able to tell that I had come back. Even taking two stairs at a time caused me to wince, so I got a taxi to save my legs. I turned right on the busy street, as the instructions I'd read online had told me, and headed for the Zoar chapel a block down.

There were twenty people waiting, mainly women in big scarves to protect against the crisp wind, all milling around in small groups. Everyone went quiet and I looked up and saw Emily.

– Good afternoon, she said, – And welcome to a walking tour with a difference. Most tours in this city are about one man in particular, who will not be named by me, as we don't know his real name. If I am to refer to him at all it will be as the Unidentified Murderer. These are matinee tours rather than evening ones, because unfortunately there isn't as much interest in this man's victims as there is in the unidentified murderer himself. Which is the wrong way round, if you ask me. And I suspect you agree, if you've come here to hear me talk.

A murmur of agreement came from the crowd. She went round from person to person as she asked for tips. One after the other, people put notes in a hat or held their phones up to a QR code on a small card she was holding in the same hand, and Emily nodded her head in thanks as she talked about the locations we would be visiting.

And then she got to me.

I already had a twenty pound note out, but before I had a chance to put the money in, she took the hat away.

She said, – What are you doing here?

– I just need a minute of your time after, I said.

– What was it you said to me again? She said. – Oh, yeah. I Don't Need Your Help.

– I was feeling vulnerable. I didn't mean to humiliate you.

– Bit late for that.

She walked into the centre of the circle. I said, – Please Emily, I really do need your help.

She didn't say anything. She just looked from person to person in the crowd, and they looked at me.

I turned in embarrassment and walked away.

6PM

I decided that toasting your long-lost thesis would make me feel better for twenty minutes. But over that drink in the Glendower, I decided that I owed it to you to find out if Emily knew anything that could help.

A couple in the booth behind me ordered fish and chips. I checked the time. I thought about ordering one myself, but then I thought if I had been walking for a couple of hours and was just given a handful of notes in tips, then the first thing I would do would be to treat myself to something delicious also.

It took me five minutes to find her in the window of a burger joint. She was sat on a bar stool, looking at her phone. A man came up to her and put a burger down that looked like it had more toppings than patty.

She didn't look up when the door tinkled as I walked in. There were a few couples sat at tables and the man who had given Emily her burger told me to go up to the counter when I was ready to order. I timed it so I sat at the stool next to her as she took her second bite.

– I just want a minute of your time, I said.

I waited for her to speak. She took her time eating, and then she said, – Go. Away.

She unfolded her cutlery from the napkin, and I wondered for a minute if I was about to get the knife in the leg, but then she put her uneaten part of the burger down.

As she started to put another napkin on top, I said, – I'm trying to do one last thing for Alexis. I need to find her thesis so her doctorate can be awarded. Do you have any ideas where it could be?

She wrapped her burger up and said, – Don't lie to me. You're not doing it for her. You're doing it for yourself. You don't know your sister at all. Now stop bothering me or I'll call the police.

– Didn't, I said. – You mean I didn't know her, not that I don't. Which is untrue anyway.

She got off the stool. I followed her out before the door could swing shut.

I ran after her and said, – What do you mean,

that I don't know my sister? Why didn't you say 'didn't'?

She turned left down a side street and said, – Slip of the tongue.

I said, – No it wasn't. You know something. Why won't you tell me?

She got her phone out and said, – That's it, I'm calling the police.

She unlocked her phone and started to dial, and I felt my chance slipping away.

I had to do something. We were on a terraced street, the doors at the pavement. A blue door next to me was newly painted, but the brass handle was bending up slightly, and not parallel to the ground. I turned it down as far as I could, then pressed it in a little and then back out.

From nowhere I saw a woman wearing a shawl leave the house, scowling. She turned around, shouting and screaming at the door, then stamped off and she was gone.

I looked at Emily. She stood there, saying nothing, phone down by her side. In the end she said, – Alexis made me swear.

– Made you swear what?

– The last time I saw her. That I would only speak with you if I knew you could do what she could.

6.30PM

The back of Central Station was full of people hurrying in and out. Emily looked at the floor and pointed at a spot and said, – Here. She told me if ever you were like her I was supposed to bring you here.

I looked around. There was a blue plaque above our heads:

> MARGED LEWIS
> 1848–1882
> DIED HERE
> MAY GOD HAVE MERCY ON HER SOUL

– I've seen these signs before, I said. – They found a Butcher of Butetown victim here.

– You make it sound like it was meant to happen, Emily said. – This isn't where she was found. It's where she was murdered.

I had no answer. I decided to smother my embarrassment in thinking about you. Then I noticed that the paving stones under our feet weren't flush, as if the labourer who put them in was trying to finish at half day. I knelt down and cleared one of dust, then dragged my hand across it.

I stepped back, and you were stood in front of us.

You were wearing the same denim jacket and black tee as when you left our house in a rush that night, and you were holding your thesis. You pointed at it, and then your left eye. Then, you crouched on one knee and pointed again and stayed still, not moving, until you disappeared.

Emily said, – I couldn't work out what was she pointing at.

I said, trying my luck, – Maybe it's what happened at that exact spot earlier. – What happened earlier was a murder.

She walked around to where Alexis had stood, then bent down and pointed. She said, – This is where Alexis was. If I stay still and point like she was doing then we can work out what she was pointing at.

A man on his phone walked out the back of the station concourse and turned right, walking away. There were a couple of people inside, but they were at a machine. I looked at Emily and said, – Are you sure you want to do this?

– We don't have much choice.

I wiped the slab again and placed my hand over it.

There were two figures walking side by side towards us. A man, in a high collared long coat partially blocking his face, was talking with a woman. As she went to say something, his hands came up. One went around her neck as another went over her mouth and nose. Her eyes went wide, and he was pressing hard, and she took a step back as she scratched at him and she fell down, but he was still holding on. Her thrashing became more sudden, and then, finally, it stopped.

Emily was standing between the man and the woman. From the inside of his coat he pulled a knife. He held the woman's head back and pressed his weight down and dragged it across her neck.

I wanted to be sick. The man stood up, wiped the knife in her clothes, and they were gone.

Emily fell down, then got up. She started to walk away. I caught up with her and said, – I have no idea why Alexis would want us to see that.

– It was because of the label.

I paused. – What do you mean?

– When I was bending down like Alexis did, I was pointing at a label on the inside hem of that woman's jacket.

– What did it say?

She looked at me. Then she got her phone out and started typing. She turned it round and showed me:

#
IA OWEN
1 WHITE STREET COWBRIDGE
#

– It was just the name of a tailor, I said. – His shop is probably a Waitrose by now. Alexis wouldn't hide her thesis behind the oat milk.

– She pointed at her eye just after the thesis. Then when I copied her and pointed down at Marged, I was pointing at the 'I' in 'IA Owen'. You'll have to believe me on this. I don't want to go through that again to check. It was traumatic.

I looked at the screen once more. I said, – I think I know.

– What is it?

– Alexis was a historian. So we have to think about what would come to her mind. Say she was pointing at the Owen. There is only one historical reference to an Owen in the whole city. It's Owain Glyndŵr, otherwise known as Owen Glendower. The pub named after him isn't far from here. I bet that's where her thesis is.

I turned to walk, but Emily stood still.

– You need to release Marged before we leave.

I stopped walking. – What do you mean, release her?

– When we were researching the events of 1882, your sister and I discovered the historical record of some murders had been removed, and re-enactments were done in their place over the years. Alexis never figured out how to let ghosts go. I saw her try so many times. But she once said that if you knew how to do this looping thing, you would be a natural. I can see that now. You're never still. And you're always doing that strumming thing with your thumb.

Emily didn't know the half of it. My whole life has been a fucked up performance. Every day I have to fight a secret war. It always used to raise your curiosity how I would control my breathing, and stare at lights to cleanse myself, and spend minutes finding a certain position for cups and plates. I wouldn't even know how to begin to explain to someone how, for instance, I have to expel the unclean air I have been breathing in a certain pattern, or my head will tell me that I have developed throat cancer. I'm so used to it by now that the staccato way I breathe is almost as natural as anyone else's steady in-and-out that they take for granted.

Every facet of it has been getting worse since your accident. But Hurley was so pissed off when Mari McBryde was released before I got beat up. And once the ghosts are gone, what they can tell us about the past is gone, too. So I said, – But researchers like Alexis might need to catalogue this in the future.

Emily said, – It's what she would have wanted.

– Don't play that one.

She sighed and said, – Think about it. If you release Marged, then no one else will be able to discover the clue. Maybe that's why Alexis was here. So you would have to release Marged after.

I thought and then thought some more. It sounded exactly like something you would do.

We went back to the spot. I looped them and before Marged could speak, I took her by the hand and walked her away. The man started to strangle thin air. Marged turned to me and smiled, and she disappeared.

7PM

The bar was three deep in places. It took me ten minutes to get served.

I said to the girl behind the bar, – I don't suppose anyone left a satchel here a few weeks ago?

She eyed me up, then told me to hold on as she got a guy about my age in a black shirt, presumably the manager. He asked me what I wanted.

When I said about the satchel he said, – We were told it belonged to a specific person.

– Levi, I said. – My name's Levi. My sister left it here.

The manager smiled and said, – Sorry, can't help you.

– Alexis? I said. – Did she just give her own name?
– No.
I thought quick. – Hurley? Mimpriss? Butcher?
– Sorry, pal.

He turned to another man and asked him what he wanted. I walked back to the door where Emily was waiting for me.

I was missing something. You wouldn't have used my name because then anyone could have picked it up. I thought back to what we saw at the rear of Central Station.

I went back to the bar. The manager was pouring a pint. I had to call out for his attention twice.

– Owen, I said. – It must be left under the name IA Owen.

– Well done, pal, he said, as he put the pint down in front of the man next to me. – We wondered if anyone would actually pick it up.

He finished serving then disappeared from the bar. I stood there for a couple of minutes watching everyone drinking and eating, wishing I had ordered that fish and chips earlier.

The manager came round my side of the bar and gave me a brown leather satchel. But before I could open it, he said, – Has this got anything to do with the lily?

I took my hand off the clasp. – What lily? I said.

– The lily on the bookies next door. Seems to be a fresh one put there all the time now. That's been the first mystery around here, then we had that girl practically begging us to look after the satchel. I thought cos they were both so unusual that they must be connected.

I thought about the bookmakers. When I was trapped in this pub and Hurley had helped me escape from Coburn and Radar, I recalled seeing a white flower stuck to the wall outside. I had no idea if it was a lily or not. So I said, – I don't think so. Sorry, mate.

I signalled to Emily and we sat down at a booth that had just been vacated. Inside the satchel was a pile of paper an inch and a half thick. They had been hole- punched and were held together with string. The front page read:

FESTIVAL OF THE GHOST – ALEXIS SILVA –
A THESIS SUBMITTED IN PARTIAL FULFILMENT OF THE REQUIREMENTS FOR THE DEGREE OF PHD IN HISTORY

You had signed the declaration on the next page. I rotated the paper onto Emily's side so she could have a look. The happiness on her face made its way onto mine. She flipped through to the contents. Then she looked through the introduction briefly and passed it over to me.

I said, – I can't wait to hand this over to her PhD supervisor.

I started to scan the page, but Emily put her hand over where I was reading. – Spend some time with it, she said. – Read all of it, then give it to him when you're ready. It's all you have left of her.

But I knew I couldn't do that. I wanted rid of it. Every page would remind me of you.

I said, – I need to get it to her supervisor ASAP. I don't need to read it. I can still loop her if I get sad.

– That's something else we have to discuss.

I told Emily not to say another word. We went outside on the pavement, and it felt cooler than it had done not fifteen minutes before. I started walking away so she would get the idea. She called out after me, but I kept walking.

8PM

We were still arguing as we got to Hurley's street. There was one light coming from his house. He opened the door within a minute of me phoning and practically dragged me in, not even noticing Emily, who stayed outside.

– What the hell are you doing? he said. – Do you know how much trouble you could bring to my door bringing her here?

I passed him the thesis without speaking. He looked at it, read the title page, and his face changed. – Oh my God, he said. – Where did you find it?

I remembered how he went off when I let Mari McBryde go. So I just said, – We missed one of the boxes. It was under the stairs all along. The woman outside was a friend of Alexis'. She helped me.

– Oh, he said, looking confused. He scratched the nick on his cheek then said, – I'll write the letter of recommendation in the morning.

I saw myself out. I was thankful that Emily had left, so I walked down the street by myself.

But one thing was still bothering me. I thought finding your thesis would mean more. I had delivered it safely after so much trouble, but it didn't make me feel any better. All I could do was walk, and hope that I felt better tomorrow.

9PM

My route home took me past the part of Bute Street where Hurley and I saw you trying to loop Mary Jane Kelly, where she was in the cafe and it felt like she was staring at me. I waited for the breeze that had blown up to still.

I stood where the corner of four pavement slabs didn't quite meet and turned to face the other way. Then a sailor came by, turned his head and smiled, and kept walking, as if he saw a girl in the cafe that used to stand here that he liked.

But it wasn't a sailor, or Mary Jane Kelly, that I wanted to see.

At one and the same time I loved and hated finding your loops. I loved it because I got to see you, but I hated it because I couldn't hear you speak, and because there was only the shimmer of life in your movements, as you were never aware of me in that space around you.

But I couldn't help myself. One of the reasons my week had been so bad was because I'd had no reason to loop you. So I used my shoe to drag out some moss from the next slab over and pressed down.

You appeared again, as Hurley and I had seen you on the day of your funeral. But then, just before you went, I swear I saw you flinch and look, like you were right in front of me, staring into my eyes.

You disappeared. There was no one around except for me and the moon. I wanted to loop you again, to see if your eyes followed me or if I was just making it up, but I knew that I couldn't. I needed to go home and put the TV on loud so it felt like I wasn't the only person in the world. But my phone rang, and the name on the screen said Hurley.

I hoped it was good news. I needed good news right then.

– Is everything OK? I said.

– It was the wrong one, he said. – It wasn't the right thesis.

I could hear him breathing down the phone. Waiting for me to speak. Waiting for me to make everything right.

– What do you mean, it was the wrong one? I said.

– I mean, a couple of pages in and it's just a standard Lorem Ipsum dummy text with Keep Safe Danger every now and again.

After all that effort. Sneaking around the place before two rhinos gave me concussion. I thought back to when I had what I thought was your thesis in my hands. I was so excited that I didn't even think to check it over, as Emily had wanted me to. I didn't even notice that the first page was different.

I said, – Did it say anything on the front? – Just her name, title, all that crap.

– No handwritten notes or anything?

– Nothing at all.

His breathing down the phone was stopping me from thinking about what I had missed at the Glendower. In the end I said, – I don't know what to say.

– You can start by saying the name of that girl you were with, he said. – And her phone number. I told you not to trust her. God, she was probably from that church. She's probably swapped that turd you gave me for the real thing.

– That's impossible.

– How do you know? he said straight away.

I had no answer.

– Christ, we'll have to visit everywhere again, he said eventually. – We must have missed something. Do you remember Shields Square, the place I took you to after I got you out of that pub? That would be a good place to start. It must be on your way home.

– I've already passed it.

He sighed and said, – Can't you go back? I have a conference coming up in Berlin and I'm not sure how much time I will have to dedicate towards this when my preparation for that gets rolling.

He insisted I text him Emily's name and number while I was still on the phone. I turned around and started to walk towards the square, feeling worse than when I'd left the house, wishing you'd never gone to university in the first place.

10PM

I was walking down the passage to Shields Square, the place Hurley asked me to go back to, when I saw two figures. It was too late for them to be builders this time. One of them swept the floor with a foot. Then he used a forearm to brush down his other arm. Then I realised, despite the dark, that the man doing the ritual was Peter Blake Turner.

I stopped walking. I went to the shadows so I couldn't be seen. What the hell were they doing here so late? Two more figures appeared in front of him. A man was strangling an older man, bringing him to the ground, and I realised I was seeing the murder that Hurley had shown me. I felt sick to my stomach.

But then Turner put his hand towards him. As he did so he twisted it round, as if he was trying to find a path through something. He reached the old man's arm and pulled him.

The old man got up from the floor. He looked down at where he had been lying, where Turner senior was butchering the thin air. Then he looked over at Turner junior himself, and lunged at his face. Turner, sensing something, moved his head back, but the old man's nails caught his face. He continued to lunge, as Turner dodged and ducked, stepping back with each attempt. Then the old man started moving backwards, as if he was being dragged away, and his lunges towards Turner turned to outreached palms, as if he was trying to grab onto something to keep himself from being taken back. Eventually, the force of whatever was pulling him was too much, and he allowed himself to be pulled and he faded and was gone.

Turner put his hand up to his cheek, and I saw his eyebrows go up and a slight smile form on his face when he saw the blood on his fingers.

– Fifteen seconds, Radar said to him. – He really went for it.

– I'm getting sloppy, Turner answered. – I hate it when they get so close.

They kept on talking, but I didn't pay much attention because I decided it was time to get out. I took a step back so I could leave the way I came, but I felt something sharp press into my lower back. A hand grabbed my shoulder. And I heard Coburn say, – Let's go have a chat.

He made me round the corner and walk into the square. Turner and Radar stopped talking when they saw me.

– How much did he see? Turner said.

– I'm not sure, Coburn answered. – I was still doing up my fly when I saw him.

Coburn walked me in front of Turner. My heart had slowed right down. It was beating strong but it felt as though it stopped every few seconds, like I was being punched in the chest.

Then Turner said, – It doesn't matter now. There's nothing more to see anyway.

He made a little dismissive, brush away-type gesture with his hand and Coburn let go of my shoulder and took a step back. I reached up and rubbed away the pain. They were stood around me, putting me in the centre of their triangle.

– We know you can do it, Radar said, eventually. – We know you can bring forth ghosts.

I thought long and hard before I answered. There was no way he could have known. Unless someone had told him. I trusted Hurley. I trusted Emily. I began to doubt myself. But I had to find out what they knew. So I said, – I don't believe in ghosts.

Turner smiled and said, – Fine. You don't believe in ghosts. So what's on my hand?

It seemed like a trick question. But I couldn't work out how. So I said, – I can't speak Latin.

The three of them laughed. Turner raised his hand.

– No one has had Latin on their palm in thirty years, he said.

There were three lines of text on his palm, unfaded. I peered closer and read:

> THE PAST
> IS WITH US
> IN THE PRESENT

I noticed some movement either side of me. I looked to my left, then to my right. Both Coburn and Radar were raising a hand. They had the same.

– He looks like his dad, see, Coburn said. – Strong genes. They could have been twins.

I wanted to bring a hand up to my temple. I didn't need Hurley or Emily to tell on me. Not that I really thought they did anyway. I had ratted on myself.

– The ability to do what we do is rare, Turner said. – And we should stick together. Our church is like a family. And that's not something you really have any more, is it, Levi? The Festival of the Ghost is nigh upon us. The feast day of our church. We could baptise you into our religion. You would never have to work another pointless job again. We control the judiciary, the media and the council. We can show you how to make sure you live a life of prosperity, both material and spiritual.

I tried not to let my face show any emotion. The

thought of what I had just seen was enough to make me sick. He had released that old man from his loop, but if there was another festival due, maybe it was only so they could re-enact another, fresher murder. With Turner Jr doing the killing this time, and not his dad. So I said, – I'll think about it.

Turner took his eyes off me after an uncomfortable second and looked over each of my shoulders. I could feel, right then, that the non-threatening part of our conversation was over.

I had to think fast. I couldn't turn and run because the two thugs either side of me would catch me in a second. I knew that at least Coburn had a blade on him, and Radar probably did too.

But when Coburn had come behind me, he had pressed the blade into the right of my spine, so that meant he was right-handed. And he was behind me to my left. Turner, with his smooth palms, looked like he had never worked a day's labour in his life. If I was going to make a break for it then it would have to be forward and left, so that Coburn would have to try and grab me with his weaker hand.

I ran forward. Turner and Coburn both lunged but I shoved Turner aside and sprinted. I could hear their feet clacking after me. I went down a passage, still running, and came out onto the busy road. I turned to look and fifty yards behind me I could see Coburn, Radar and Turner half jogging, half marching.

I knew I would be safe if I stuck to this street. It was too busy with a constant stream of passing cars for them to attempt anything. On my side a Turkish barber was still open, with two guys outside vaping, yet to have their turn in the chair. I kept my pace for another couple of minutes, passing full bus stops and darting between the leaning souped-up bikes of food delivery guys waiting to pick up orders from fried chicken shacks, and when my gasps for air became uncontrollable, I stopped.

But they were still there, right behind me.

I wouldn't try to hide this time. I ran through the traffic across the road. I had to have a plan. I thought about running to Hurley's, but it wouldn't be fair to get myself looped outside his front door. So I put my arm out for a taxi and jumped in. The driver asked me where to, and I said the first place that entered my head.

9 APRIL

10AM

The minute it got light enough for me to see through the trees, I gave up trying to sleep. I tried ringing Emily when the hour became sociable, and she texted me to meet her outside a sandwich shop near the university.

By the time I had walked back into the city to the small workman's cafe that looked more like a hardware shop, she was already outside waiting for me.

She said, – Sorry for missing your calls. That was a dick move.

I told her it was fine. I thanked her for coming to see me. It all felt so formal. Then she said, – I'm not here for you. I'm here for Alexis.

And I said, – Me too.

She broke the silence by saying, – It's too busy to do it now. If we come back after dark it should be quiet.

– Do what? I said.

Something dawned in her face. She said, – What did you think we were doing?

– The thesis we found was fake, I said. – It was pure gibberish after the first few pages. We must have missed something. I wanted to ask you to help me go through everything again so we can find the right one.

– Do you know where we're stood? She said. – Do you know the significance of this place?

There wasn't much to this street. A row of buildings from the eighties, a few bookies, and the sounds of drills and demolition.

I shook my head.

Emily said, – This is where Alexis was run over. I thought you were here to free her from her loop.

It was the last thing I wanted. Especially now.

I said, – I can't release her until the thesis is found.

– Have you considered, she said, eyes pursed, – That maybe Alexis never wanted it found?

– That's rubbish, I said, perhaps a little too fast. – It was obviously a double bluff. I bet we missed something down at the Glendower. She wanted me to find it. I can feel it.

She said, – Once you've found it, will you release her?

I said nothing. Verbalising that one word, we both knew, was going to change everything.

– You can't do it, Emily said. – You won't do it. Even if you do manage to find that thesis, it's not going to do anything for you. Ever wonder why she was so distant from you lately? She was protecting you. And now you won't even do one last thing for her and lay her to rest. I won't be a part of it.

I thought about telling her how when I was on the street near our house where Mary Jane Kelly's cafe once stood and I looped you, it felt like you looked at me yesterday. But Emily walked away. I felt like going after her, but I knew it would be pointless.

And I had my own prerogative anyhow. I had to go down to the Glendower, and find what I'd missed.

1 PM

It was lunchtime, and though I loved a good pub, I was gutted I lived in a city of alcoholics. The booths were all full, and the bar busy with lunchtime drinkers, with a steady stream of people going back and forth to the toilets like ants.

I had the feeling that you wouldn't have done this to me. You would never have expected me to loop and cause a scene.

I drank my pint quickly and left. Outside on my right was the chalked-out pavement area where the Glendower's smokers were ruining their cardiovascular fitness. But to my left, next to the pub and just about opposite the church, there was that quiet corner outside the boarded up bookmakers, out of the warmth of the sun.

Something caught my eye. I walked up to the shopfront and there, next to the wooden chipboard where a window had once been, was a single white flower, stuck to the wall.

I thought back to what the bar manager had said last night. I did a quick double-check behind me, then rubbed an annoying smudge on the chip and blew out the air from the bottom of my lungs.

You appeared in front of me. You were pointing at yourself and shaking your head. Though I knew this was just an animation, it felt like you were looking directly at me, as if you were trying to tell me something. You were holding a pile of paper in your other hand, but not the satchel. You were pointing at yourself and your eyes were pleading. It was as if you didn't want me to do something for once. You kept shaking your head and then you were gone.

I needed to dig deeper. I needed to think harder. I needed, more than anything, for Emily to tell me what you were thinking.

If I wasn't meant to look at you, who was I supposed to look at?

There was a missing tile on the front of the Glendower where it met the bookmakers. Pattern breaks like this always manifested an almost physical pain in me. I positioned my hand so the space where the tile had gone was covered by my palm. It was almost as if I could feel the energy and goodness being taken from my body, so I took it away and squeezed my palm shut.

Nothing happened. I must have had it wrong.

Then I turned round.

There was a couple kissing in front of me. The woman was wearing a short red dress and she had henna hair. The man had a shaved head and was brown, maybe African or West Indian in heritage. He pulled away and smiled. They looked at each other.

The woman was Jayne Mimpriss, your other PhD supervisor. They held hands, and walked towards the Glendower's entrance.

Was this really what you wanted me to see? Not the Butcher, nor one of his unfortunate victims, but a professor and her boyfriend? It didn't make any sense.

I looked around but felt nothing. I had already seen you at your old house with her, and Mimpriss had told me herself about your disagreement in the kitchen over whether it was the Butcher or a bunch of squaddies who had killed Mari McBryde.

But she never told me if you had resolved the debate. Or even why she refused to accept your thesis in the first place.

I would have to see for myself if you had shown her how you actually knew it was the Butcher who had killed Mari.

Ten minutes later and I was down the damp alley where Mari had been killed. There was no one around. I straightened my back, then arched forwards just enough until it felt right, and kicked the wall.

You appeared in front of me. You were tugging on your ear and then you put a cigarette on the cobbles, parallel to the newbuild flats.

You stepped back and looked up. I was glad that I never had to see what you were watching. Then your head turned and it was as if you were looking at me. But out of the corner of my eye, I noticed that I hadn't seen what was nearby.

You weren't looking at me, but the people who were with you. The people to whom you were showing the death of Mari McBryde.

There, looking up at the wall, was Jayne Mimpriss. She was holding hands with the man I had seen her kissing outside the Glendower. She was rubbing the cross on her necklace, as I had seen her in her do in her office when she got nervous, as the man slowly raised his hand over his mouth.

You disappeared, leaving me feeling lonely and lost and in need of answers.

I looked at my phone. It was a quarter to three. Mimpriss knew more than she was letting on. I had plenty of time to get to the university before she left her office.

3PM

The students were letting themselves through the turnstiles with cards. I thought about pretending that I'd lost mine, but I couldn't for the life of me remember which room, or even which floor, Mimpriss was on. In the end I went up to the security guard and said, – I have an appointment with Professor Jayne Mimpriss in the History department.

He looked me up and down. He read through a clipboard with his finger.

– She isn't expecting any visitors today, he said. – What's your name, please? I said, – Peter Blake Turner.

He opened a folder and typed a four digit number into a landline. He started talking, but I could barely hear him over the constant beeps of the cards and the clanking of turnstiles when the students gained entry.

The guard was saying Yes into the phone every few seconds. He was looking at me as he did this. Then he put the phone down, said room 236 and pointed me to the lift.

I heard no noise, but knocked once and let myself in. Mimpriss was leaning forward, with her hands on the desk, her fingers intertwined as if she was in prayer. When she realised I wasn't Turner, she leaned back in the chair and sighed.

– You think that's funny, do you? she said. – I'm going to call security. I said, – I'll only be a second. I need your help with a few questions.

She picked up her phone and pressed a button. I wondered how long it would take the guard to climb two flights of stairs. I said, – You were lying to me before about your argument in Alexis' kitchen. I know she showed you how Mari McBryde was killed and how it was actually the Butcher who did it and not a bunch of pissed-up Squaddies.

Mimpriss stared at me. She put the phone down and gestured for me to sit.

She didn't say anything, clearly waiting for me to speak. So I said, – I'm still looking for the thesis. I know you told me not to but this is something I have to do for her. Alexis showed you the murder along with another man. Someone you used to meet at the Glendower.

Mimpriss leaned back in her chair again. She said, – He was your sister's secondary supervisor. We used to meet there every Sunday. He died in an accident a few months ago.

I said, – But I thought you were her second.

– I was her primary. Gwyn Covey was her second. Then my colleague Dr Ted Hurley became her supervisor after I had to take time off. It was a de facto role, though. She was so close to the end that all he had to do was sign a few things and make sure she was prepped for the viva.

Now it was my turn to be silent. Hurley had never mentioned a Gwyn Covey before. But then he never had a need to. I thought about asking Mimpriss how he died, but I wasn't sure, from how her shoulders were up, if she could even tell me. So I said, – Could there be a copy of the thesis in Dr Covey's stuff?

– Look, Levi, it's really about time you dropped this. Forget about the thesis, before something bad happens.

I said nothing.

In the end I said, – Is that a threat?

She laughed and said, – Sorry, sorry. It's just that you don't know what danger you're in. All I'll say to you is you should really leave it alone, unless you want to end up like your sister or mother.

My heart went slow. I felt the blood leave my body. I said, – What do you mean, end up like my mother? What do you mean?

She was already picking up the phone. I said, – What do you mean? What do you mean?

She spoke into the phone and put it down. I said hang on now you can't say something like that about my mum and not explain more and I got up and I didn't know what to do but I had to let her know that she couldn't do this, and I went around to her side of the desk and I was saying What do you mean? What do you mean? But the security guard came bursting through the door and he grabbed me around the arms and picked me up, and I kicked out and almost got Mimpriss in the face but the guard marched me out of the room and I heard the door slam and a lock click and he shoved me as we walked down the fire escape.

The whole time I was telling him that I had to get back in there, I had to speak to her. But he just said that he was about to call the police.

He slammed the doors shut. I was in an alley next

to some bins. I thought of calling Hurley but I had no time to waste.

I had to get back home. I had to see for myself.

5PM

This is what I wanted to see. I wanted to see Mum tripping down the stairs and landing at the bottom. Then, dazed from the fall and running on autopilot, I wanted to see her noticing the mess she had made with the blood and instead of ringing for help from the house phone next to the front door, I wanted to see her going to the kitchen, finding a cloth and cleaning up her own blood, even while more blood dripped from her head as she was cleaning. Finally I wanted to see signs in her movements of her brain haemorrhaging from the damage and then her collapsing, and then maybe another loop of me finding her a couple of hours later when I got back from the call centre.

I walked up the stairs. I wanted to see Mum lose her footing. I didn't want what Mimpriss said to be true.

On the landing, I noticed that the carpet weave was all facing the wrong way. I smoothed it down with my foot, then shut the bathroom door and opened it just a smidge so that I could see through into the mirror. Then I brought my fingers down on the door, knocked once, and stepped back.

Mum came out of the bedroom. She was looking tired, rubbing her eyes, and was in her light blue dressing gown, the one she always wore. It had been five years since I had seen her and she looked younger somehow, and then I realised that I was getting older. I had to get out of her way as she walked past me. Then as she got to the top of the stairs, still looking half asleep, a figure emerged at the bathroom. I recognised it at once as Radar. He stepped forward just as she took her first step. His hand came up, the one with the tattoo, and he shoved her hard.

Mum's head lolled backwards, and the rest of her body went forward, and she missed half a dozen steps. As I looked over the bannister I saw her head bounce at the bottom. I could practically hear the crack of it hitting the floor. I raced down the stairs. As I got close I stopped. She was lying on her back. She was looking up at the ceiling and muttering but her eyes were unfocussed.

I wanted to help. I wanted to see if her spirit was trapped in the loop. But as I put my hand out to feel, I noticed something to my left.

Out of nowhere I saw Coburn. Something in Mum made her notice him too, but she couldn't move anything but her eyes. He picked her head up and cracked it as hard as he could on the floor. Blood started oozing out over the tiles. He picked her head up again and smashed it into the ground one last time.

I had never hated anyone more.

Then he turned her round, and put a damp cloth in her hand. He made her clean the floor with it, her still, limp fingers doing nothing. Then he lay her down, face on her hand and blood coming through her hair, and stepped away.

I wanted to call the police. I wanted to tell them what these two men had done to my mother. I would bring the whole thing down, the entire church and fuck what would happen to me. I could bring a detective here and show him what I could do and maybe even work for the police myself, becoming the best crime scene analyst that the world had ever known.

But deep down I knew this wouldn't work. It would be suicide. They would have to arrest every member of the church. If they put me in witness protection, the Spiritists would still be able to get to me, because the church knew how to find everything out about everyone. They could blackmail every single officer involved in looking after me if they wanted to. I dreaded to think what kind of power Turner had over certain people, and who the church held in their pocket.

I started crying. But I knew this wasn't the end. I still had a job to do. As Radar made his way down the stairs and used the banister to swing over Mum's body, I pushed my hand through and found a path and picked her up.

I was stood facing her. A small smile broke out on her face. She threw her arms around me. For the smallest second I felt a squeeze, as if she was here and giving me a hug once more, as if she wasn't murdered but alive. But when I opened my eyes, she wasn't there.

I sat on the bottom stair and held my head in my hands, and I stayed that way, thinking of you both, and daring Coburn and Radar to come and find me, until it got dark.

10 APRIL

8AM

At daybreak I woke and downed a pint of water. The sun hadn't quite got to the horizon, giving the sky and the light a distinctly blue hue.

I took my phone off flight mode. On a PDF on the council website, I found the minutes of the last planning session Mum had attended. She had flat out refused to sanction the building of the Spirit Freedom Centre, and I took pride that she had held her ground. Then I checked the council's press releases, and saw that it had been finally granted, in what was deemed a 'surprising' move, a month after her death.

When I was leaving the house, I couldn't find the right jig to get the door to lock. I put it down to tiredness, and tried to make myself not get frustrated. I thought it wouldn't hurt to try the spare key I kept under one of the plant pots you got for the house once. But when I found it I noticed that the round fob wasn't in line with the actual ribbed part of the key.

I knew I hadn't done this. Sure, I had come back drunk many a time. Once, I remember, I couldn't get my key in the lock no matter how hard I tried, and I ended up sleeping on the doorstep until you woke me up in the early hours of the morning, but I had never bent a key out of shape like this before.

And then a thought hit me. Someone had been in the house.

I felt around. I pushed the lock in as much as I could. Then I breathed out and stepped back.

Hurley appeared in front of me. He was wearing a black blazer and his shirt with the big collar, just like when I first met him at your funeral. He was standing on one leg and he put a penny on the floor. Then he stepped back, looked around, and went for the key under the plant pot.

For fuck's sake, I thought. I knew on the day of your funeral that I hadn't left the door open when he walked in. He didn't have to lie about it.

I watched as the looped Hurley put the key in the lock and jiggled it about. I could see the anger rising in his face. Then he hammered at the key with the side of his fist and I saw it bend. He wiped his sweaty face with his forearm and I noticed the small cut on his cheekbone. Finally he hit the door with his hip and it opened, and he put the key back and was gone.

It really pissed me off that Hurley had lied to me. At least, I thought, he didn't have an easy time of it, sweating as he was.

But a detail of it wasn't quite right. I couldn't explain to myself why, but I had to see him do it again. So I opened and shut the door, then pulled it even tighter shut until it felt comfortable to me. Then I pressed down on the handle and stepped back.

Hurley was repeating his ritual again, up on one foot. I looked at his face.

It was the nick on his cheekbone.

There was no way he had that cut at your funeral. His girlfriend had given him that when I went to his house, I remembered him telling me not to mention it. This was a more recent attempt.

But why would he want me to think he was breaking in when I first met him, when I came back here early at your funeral? I had so many questions.

9.15AM

I decided to wait for Hurley by the bike stands, giving me a good view of the entrance without looking suspicious. But I had no idea if he was the kind of academic who started early and finished while the sun was still up, or if he was the type who rolled into the department at eleven and relied on his track record to carry him through.

I thought about how many times you must have stood where I now was, locking and unlocking your bike. A green one had lost its back tyre, and another had been stripped of almost everything down to the frame, even the forks. I couldn't handle the way it was discarded, sitting at an uncomfortable angle to the iron stand it was locked to. I picked it up so it was leaning against the metal, and brushed some dirt off it, then wiped my hand on my trousers.

I leaned on one of the stands. Then I realised I wasn't alone.

You were standing in front of me. You were putting on a helmet, but as you did up the strap you looked behind you. Then you threw it down and undid your bike lock instead. Your hands were shaking. You jumped on your bike and started pedalling, and you were gone.

I needed to have it out with Hurley. But something was telling me that I had to see where you were leading me.

I walked up the street, and as I got to the side of one of the old listed villas that had had been turned into university offices, I felt uncomfortable with how it was all set out. I looked over, and on the road sat a big, blue wheelie bin. Only the back wheel was touching the kerb, so I pushed the front one so it was also against it and dusted off my hands.

You appeared on your bike again. You were cycling fast past me, but as you turned to go into the street you looked to your right and opened your mouth to shout and put your hand out, and a large black Range Rover came from nowhere and knocked into your side. The Range Rover stopped, and you were thrown into the air by the bonnet. Your bike stayed low. You tumbled once around and smashed against the road and rolled, your arms not even coming up for protection.

Not this. Anything but this.

I could feel my anger building. I could feel the anxiety rising with every beat of my heart, in that there was nothing I could do about what I was seeing. But mostly I felt the pain of it. The total sorrow of what had happened to you had caught me, and dragged me down into the cold, dark earth.

The driver's door opened, and out stepped Coburn.

I wanted to attack him right then and there. I wanted to bunch my fingers together and poke his eyes out. But he walked slowly towards you and out of the passenger seat came Radar, holding some kind of white sheet, strutting without a care in the world. They stood over your battered broken body, then Radar wrapped the sheet around you, and Coburn walked back and got the bike and threw it in the boot. Radar put you on top of it, then they jumped into their seats and were gone.

I knew that I had seen enough. I didn't need to see any more. I just needed to go somewhere quiet and think. I needed to think about you, I needed to speak to Hurley, I needed to tell Emily. But I wouldn't be able to do any of that until I had finished your journey.

Until I had finished your murder.

I walked down the road till I got as far as the roadside cafe that Emily had taken me to when she wanted me to unloop you. I had to wait near twenty minutes until there was no one around. The whole time I stood still, hearing my breathing and getting madder and madder at what Coburn and Radar had done to you. After two men in suits walked past, I crushed down a can in the gutter and clicked my neck both ways.

Coburn and Radar appeared in front of me again, on opposite sides of their parked Range Rover. Coburn at the bonnet, Radar at the boot. They were facing the road. Radar was holding your bike. Coburn had you wrapped between his legs. I could see your blood beginning to pool through the sheet.

Coburn pointed something out, and they bent down low. He started unwrapping you. An artic lorry appeared. The driver was too high in the cab to see. As the lorry went past, Radar threw under your bike. Then Coburn threw you under, and when you started tumbling I looked the other way.

I wanted to head to the market and get a knife right there and then. But I needed answers from Hurley. So I walked slowly back towards the university, wiping the tears from my eyes.

10AM

I thought I had timed it right. But when I tried to follow a young Chinese student through the gates, an arm came out and stopped me from walking.

I looked up and saw the security guard who'd thrown me out of Mimpriss' office.

– Not a chance, he said. – This is trespass. Leave the grounds before I call the police.

I had no time for this.

– I need to speak to Dr Ted Hurley in the History department, I said. – He's a friend of mine.

– Nice try. Phone him and get him to meet

you down here. He will have to sign you in and be responsible for you.

I sighed and found his number on my phone. The call went to his answerphone. I tried again and the security guard smirked and said, – Just as I thought.

I tried once more. The phone rang but he didn't answer. Another security guard, an older, fatter one, came through the gates and asked if everything was OK. The other guard said everything was under control. I headed back down the stairs and heard them both laughing.

There was only one thing for it. Considering he had already broken into my house without my consent, I had no problem doing the same to him. I phoned him again and when it got to answerphone I told him to meet me at his place as soon as he got the message.

10.45AM

I looked at the keypad. I polished off the keys clockwise three times, then kicked the door gently and stepped back.

Hurley appeared in front of me. He was leaning against the wall. His shirt buttons were undone down past his chest and he was breathing heavily. His eyes were half-closed, as if he was looking through his eyelashes. He brought his finger up unsteadily, and pressed the number one. Then he pressed eight twice in quick succession, and missed the number two once before getting it and hitting enter. Then he fell through his own front door and was gone.

I shook my head. I looked around, dialled in the code, and walked in.

After shutting the door quietly I listened out for his girlfriend, but I couldn't hear a thing. I walked up the step to the lounge area and sat down on the sofa. I was about to phone him again when my own phone rang.

Before I could say hello, Hurley said, – What the hell are you doing? Get away from the front of my house. Meet me in the Glendower. They'll never loop us there.

I said. – I'm not waiting outside. I'm sat down on your sofa.

– What? How did you get in?

– I looped you when you were looking the worse for drink. A curious code, 1882. Wasn't that the year of the Butcher murders?

– I'm a historian. Of course it is. But that's not the point. You're out of order, Levi. You should never use this skill to break into people's houses, for Christ's sake. What were you thinking? It's the middle of the day.

– I could say the same about you when you broke into my place wearing your funeral clothes.

The line went silent. I heard him breathing, and then he said, – How did you know?

– The nick on your cheekbone. Your girlfriend gave you that the week after.

He breathed a sigh. – That was a mistake, he said. – I'm terribly sorry for my poor judgement. It's just that you weren't getting any closer to finding the thesis and I wanted to do all I could to help find it.

– By breaking into my house.

– Look, that's not the important thing right now. I break into your house, you break into mine, but the important thing is, have you found it yet?

– That's not why I'm here. I found out Coburn and Radar murdered my mother and sister.

There was silence down the line again. And then he said, – Are you sure?

– I looped them myself. They weren't accidents. They were just made to look like that.

After another pause, Hurley said, – I don't think that should be reason enough not to find the thesis.

– Did you not listen to what I just said?

He sighed and said, – These are powerful, dangerous people. They can silence individual detectives with blackmail or threat, of course, but they would probably silence you first. And it wouldn't be difficult to track you down. But searching for the thesis will give you some kind of direction and ensure that you do nothing brash. It appears counter-intuitive but it's just about the best thing you can do for yourself at this moment in time.

I knew he was right in a way. A sane person might have pretended they didn't see anything and got on with their lives. But at this moment in time, I wasn't a sane person. I couldn't care less about your thesis. He seemed to care more about it than what had happened to you.

– I don't give a shit what happens to me, I said. – Fuck the thesis. I want Coburn and Radar.

After a spell of silence, he said, – I know you're upset, but your mother and Alexis will always be with you. Don't forget that the past is with us in the present. Look, I have a seminar. Stay right there and I'll be over very soon.

– You mean, you'll be back to tell me to search for the thesis, I said.

I ended the call. I sat there in the chair, wondering about that phrase he had just said. It struck me that I had heard it before, but I couldn't work out where. I received a text from Hurley telling me not to leave.

I decided to use his toilet in the en suite upstairs. After I finished, I found myself lost in thought while staring at the bed in there. It was slightly off again. I started to nudge it with my foot. But that weird thing Hurley said about the past being in the present was all I was really thinking about. I swear I'd heard it somewhere.

And then it dawned on me, at the same time I moved the bed back into place.

I had to tense every muscle in my legs, starting at my toes. At the foot of the bed, a man appeared. He was sat down at a loom, quietly fuming, wiping the sweat from his forehead. I had never seen a more angry man, and I found myself intimidated by a man long dead.

I had seen him before, I knew it. In this exact same spot, the first time I came into this house. But I had also seen him strangle a man, and slit a woman's throat, though his face was often partially hidden behind a high collar on a long coat.

But you couldn't hide that kind of ferocity of action or violence of intent, whether you were working at a loom or cutting someone open. Anger and disdain and hatred of life makes itself known and the man I was looking at had these qualities in abundance. For the man I was looking at was the Butcher of Butetown.

11 AM

In the kitchen, there was a block of knives on the counter. I took out the middle one and tucked it in my belt. I looked down and all around. No one would know it was there.

I was about to leave when I heard a noise from the other side of the front door. The fear made me freeze. But I still had the element of surprise, so I took the stairs three at a time and hid at the top.

I looked over the bannister when I heard the door open, and Coburn and Radar walked in without saying a word. They swarmed forward. Radar went to the living room and Coburn looked in the cupboard under the stairs.

I knew hiding would be no good. They could track me down to the most remote place on Earth. Instead I breathed in and tried to keep my cool. Then I went into the bedroom and sneaked out onto the balcony, careful to make sure that the sliding doors didn't screech. I climbed onto the iron railings, refusing to look down. I reached over and grabbed at the gutter and hoisted myself onto the roof.

The breeze went straight down my back and I felt all alone, looking down, as if the straight edges of what I had known about the world no longer existed. I stuck close to the tiles and prayed none would slip. I climbed sideways over the roofs towards the main road, using chimney stacks when I could, hoping that the kids in the school behind me didn't start shouting.

Someone had turned the last roof on the corner, which was flat, into a garden of shrubs and potted plants. I walked down two flights of dingy metal stairs, until I was in a darkened yard not more than ten feet across. There was only one door at the bottom, and I walked in and found myself between stacks of metal shelves, full of chick peas and saffron and flour. I walked through, let myself out of a door, and found myself in a shop.

The man behind the till didn't even look up from his phone. I walked quickly out and found myself on the corner of Hurley's street and the busy main road. I marched quickly up it, past the school and the entrance to the car park where I had been trapped before. Then I crossed the road and rounded the corner and marched up the leafy street to the Spirit Freedom Centre.

I had to see it for myself. There was no one at the

desk. I knew I didn't have long. I took the knife out of my belt and positioned it on the desk so that the blade was facing towards the door. Then I blew on it and straightened my back.

Turner's dad was stood before me. He was wearing a grey suit and his sideburns were long, but otherwise he could have been his son. He was raising his hand as men and women walked past him, showing their own tattoos also. Then a young boy, no older than fifteen, didn't raise his hand and instead spoke to him. Turner senior pointed at the desk, and they were gone.

I had to see again, to make sure. I swept the desk top and banged hard on it with both fists and stepped back.

The younger Turner was in front of me now. He too was greeting people, as his father had, in an almost identical suit, but he had no sideburns. His hand came up every time someone came up to him and he said something and I saw his tattoo. Then a man came up and as he raised his hand Turner smiled, and he gave the man a hug. They pulled apart and he patted the man on the back. The man was faced away from me, but when he turned to walk away I saw that it was Ted Hurley himself.

I felt my legs go weak. Then I heard a clip-clopping noise from down a corridor. I walked to the exit, let myself out and walked back down the street, unsure of what was going on and who I could trust.

11.45AM

My phone rang. It was Hurley.

We stayed there in a hung silence, neither willing to speak first, till eventually he said, – They're not going to stop coming for you, you know. No matter what. So you can either meet me, and just me, to have a chat, or you can take your chances. Trust me, I know what is in your best interests.

The last sentence came out slowly and surely, not a hint of threat. More fearful than anything.

I thought fast and said, – Meet me outside St Dyfrig's.

On the way there, I was the dickhead who refused to move to the side of the pavement so people had to walk past me. A food delivery guy cycled past and I told him to get on the fucking road. One woman with a pram had to stop and almost go in the gutter between two parked cars. When I got to St Dyfrig's, I ruined someone's picture for their socials as I walked straight through their shot, but I didn't care. All I could do was stare at Hurley.

He was on one of the lower steps, scarf on,

looking down. Coburn and Radar weren't anywhere to be seen.

Before I even had a chance to say anything, he said, – You'll have to take me on my word, but I'm not who you think I am.

– I know exactly who you are, I said.

He shook his head. – Why do you think I asked you to go to Shields Square that night, when you found the fake thesis? I thought it was your best chance of survival. Turner wanted you killed, but I convinced him to try and convert you. I didn't want any of this. When your sister started enquiring about the Spiritists, Peter Blake Turner had Gwyn Covey killed so I could be in a position of responsibility. I was supposed to guide her away from the church. And I really tried. Then when it was clear that my efforts weren't working, Turner ordered her murder. It was nothing to do with me.

I had two words for him. – Bull. Shit.

– I'm not lying. Trust me, the consequences of the Spiritists not getting that thesis are as grave for me as they are for you. I have been asked to tell you that you have two days to deliver it.

I made a scoffing noise. – If the consequences are just as bad for you, then maybe if I find it I'll post it second class.

– I wouldn't if I were you.

He held out his hand. He was holding his phone. I squinted and made out a shape. I was looking at a picture of Emily. It was taken with a flash so she must have been in a dark room. She was tied to a chair, a gag in her mouth.

I swiped for his phone, but he drew it back quick and said, – Don't be daft. You think we're not being watched? The Festival of the Ghost is on April the twelfth. You have two days. If the thesis – the last loose end – isn't delivered to me or Turner at Shields Square by nine o'clock, Emily will take part in it. I wish you luck.

With that he turned and walked down the steps. I felt like following him, like pushing him down the last few and saying fuck him and fuck the Spiritists, but I knew that would mean something very bad for Emily.

Instead I remembered what he said about being watched, and walked as fast as I could down the street. I needed to get on a bus or a train, to get off each and every stop and then back on again so that my path couldn't be traced. It would mean losing valuable time, but at least going through the process would help me think.

4.30PM

I decided to work backwards. The city workers were already beginning to fill up inside the Glendower. I was outside at the quieter corner, near the old white lily, where I had last looped you. There was no one around. I rubbed my hands together and breathed into my palms, and you appeared in front of me. You were pretending to hold a necklace, in the same nervy way that Mimpriss did. But I still couldn't work out what I was missing.

I was working backwards, so I looped Mimpriss once more. And again she appeared in front of me, and the man I now know as Gwyn Covey came up to her. But as he went in to kiss her, with the biggest smile I had seen on anyone's face in a long while, I noticed her hands as they came up to either side of his face. Or, more specifically, her palms.

There was no tattoo. I looped her again, just to make sure. This time I went around the back of her, as she was holding her hands behind her back when she was waiting. Definitely clear.

I had it wrong all along. Her threats weren't malicious. They were warnings.

6.30PM

I was soaked through by the time Mimpriss left her office. I followed her all the way into the station, and she swiped with her card and I followed. When she sat down I managed to get the seat next to her. She didn't even notice.

The doors closed and the train pulled off. I had two minutes before we got to Queen Street, another two before we got to Cathays. The man to my left had his headphones in. I leaned over and quietly said to her, – I think Alexis wanted you to help me.

She looked at me, and I saw the colour drain from her face. I thought she was going to get straight up, but instead she said, – Stay. Away. From. Me.

We were silent for a second, while I worked out if anyone was pretending to scroll through their phones but actually filming us. When I decided it was clear, I said, – I saw what happened to my mother. I can't let them get away with that.

– You don't have much of a choice. If you knew what was good for you, then you would stay well away from the city, and well away from me.

– They can't see us on the train. The logistics don't work out. They would have to jump on a train and hope it was doing the exact same speed and even then they wouldn't even have a split second to feel what was wrong to get the loop to enact at the exact same spot.

She was silent. I was sure I felt her relax. But she stayed looking forwards and said, – I'm not willing to take the chance.

I said, – Please. Alexis' thesis was very important. Please help me find it.

She turned to me and said, – Why do you think it's important?

– Because it reveals the identity of the Butcher of Butetown, whom the Spiritists worship. And she wanted them exposed and his real name revealed.

She laughed so much that she leaned forward out of her seat. The guy in the headphones looked at her.

– I'm sorry, she said. – I don't mean to be so rude. Yes, your sister knew his real name. She makes an excellent case for it in one of her chapters. But can you imagine that being enough to motivate her? You didn't know her very well if you do. She was of the view that his 'real name' is the fake persona that he used to go undetected through society. The only people who knew his real identity were the men and women that he murdered. Any other details about him, as far as she was concerned, were irrelevant. Her thesis was actually a damning indictment of Peter Blake Turner and the cult of the Spiritists. She wanted to bring them down and end their cruel, violent practices, probably because she found out what happened after your mother repeatedly refused their planning application on safety grounds. That's why the Spiritists are after the thesis, and for no other reason.

Mimpriss sat back in her chair and faced forward again. No one looked up from their phones.

The tannoy announced that we were approaching Queen Street. I had to think fast. I said, – We can't be sat at the same seat at a station or they'll be able to loop us. I'll head into the next carriage and I'll be back in a second. Please, I haven't finished.

But Mimpriss leaned over to me and said, – The Spiritists have killed your sister and your mother. They killed my soul partner. They'll be coming for you, next. I have no desire to be a part of that.

The train stopped and the doors slid open. Mimpriss got up. As she crossed onto the platform I said, – I need your help. They have one of Alexis' friends. They say if I don't find the thesis they'll kill her in the festival.

She turned around and said, – I'm afraid it's already too late for her.

She walked away as the doors closed.

7PM

The hours were counting down. Mimpriss wouldn't help, Emily couldn't help, and you were a dead end. I couldn't work out who I was meant to turn to.

Then I realised. There was one person who knew your thesis pretty well who I hadn't yet consulted.

Someone had taken my seat, so I leaned by the door and got my phone out and typed in Gwyn Covey. Underneath the first two results – his university page, still up, and his Wikipedia entry – was a headline stating, University Lecturer's Tragic Death Was Accident, Coroner Rules.

Between pictures of a smiling Gwyn Covey, and appropriate obituaries from his friends and colleagues, was the supposed story of his death: he had been walking home from a night out when he stumbled and fell through the window of a bookmakers. Shards from the window had slit his neck. Others were embedded in his stomach. He was four times the legal drink drive limit, and he had bled out before anyone found him.

The last picture at the bottom showed the scene of the accident. The window was boarded up, and the pavement outside was covered in flowers. But on the wall, between the chipboard and the next unit, was a single white lily.

8PM

A few tour groups went past, and eventually, after half an hour of waiting, I brushed the chipboard where the window of the bookies was boarded, and stepped back.

Gwyn Covey was walking past me. His hands were in his pockets. But then out of nowhere Radar appeared from behind him, smothering his huge arms over Covey's own, and picked him up. Covey started to thrash out with his head and legs. But it was no good. Radar just held him there, crushing him. Coburn appeared and took his time looking around. He had something in his hand. He raised it up to Covey's collar and I could see that it was a syringe. He brought the needle close and injected it into Covey's neck.

Covey grimaced and shouted. But then his legs stopped thrashing and hung limp, and his mouth started opening slower as his eyes dimmed. I had never seen anyone look so drunk in my life. Then Radar swung Covey back briefly, bracing himself, and threw Covey where the chipboard now was.

He smashed through into the shop. Coburn climbed through after. I thought they were gone, but then Coburn climbed back out, and took off some gloves covered in blood, and put them in a bag that Radar was holding.

I felt nauseous. I was getting tired of seeing the destruction these two men were causing. And this didn't tell me anything I didn't know already.

I looked at the lily as I pondered through what

I had just seen. It was old, with its petals almost all fallen off. And then it hit me.

I walked straight up to the bar in the Glendower. The manager, the man in the black shirt, asked me what he could get me.

– Do you know when the lily outside gets changed? I said.

– The what?

– The lily on the bookies next door. You told me a couple of days ago when I picked up a satchel that someone keeps putting a fresh one there.

– Ah, the lily again. I don't know. Probably every week or so.

– Do you know what day?

He stopped and thought. – Probably a Sunday. It always looks fresh on a Monday morning when I'm out doing the barrels.

I knew, then, that I had a gamble to make.

12 APRIL

6.30PM

I had my back turned and my hood up. I was pretending to look at the menu in the window of a Bengali curry house so Mimpriss didn't notice me when she got to the boarded-up window. I watched in the vague reflection of the glass as she pinned the lily to the wall, and I walked over. She stepped back, and I stepped up to the flower and smoothed down the tape so it was perfectly stuck in the middle, and I tensed my calf muscles.

As Mimpriss went to say something, the ghost of Gwyn Covey appeared. He had his hands in his pockets again, as on his last night. Mimpriss opened her eyes wide and stared. Radar grabbed Gwyn from behind and picked him up, and Mimpriss' face turned to despair. But before Radar could administer the syringe, I pushed my hand through and grabbed Gwyn Covey by the shoulder and pulled him out.

He was standing in front of me. He looked over and saw Mimpriss. There were tears in her eyes. He went over and gave her a hug, and her body squeezed as she found his and for a second I could see there was a touch. Then he let her go, and he looked at me and nodded, and he walked away.

The tears came thick and instant.

– I don't ever want to have to do that because of them for anyone ever again, I said.

Mimpriss wiped the tears from her eyes. – How did you know? She said.

– The colour white, I said. – Gwyn can mean white, and lilies are white. And they're the flowers of sorrow and loss.

And then she said, – We have a lot to talk about.

8PM

Mimpriss insisted on reviewing the evidence, so we wasted time going around to each site and seeing what you had done and where you had led me. But our journey brought forth nothing new except for some soreness to the soles of my feet. I was constantly looking over my shoulder to make sure we weren't being followed, but it wouldn't have made a difference anyway. They wanted the thesis, not me.

The last stop was back at the Glendower. We waited till some smokers had gone inside, then I coughed twice and turned around, and brushed both shoulders.

You appeared in front of us. It was as if you were watching, as if you were there in front of us and you weren't dead. You shook your head and held an imaginary necklace in front of your neck and rubbed it, just like Mimpriss did, and then you were gone.

– How does this work again? Mimpriss said. – How do we work out what she meant?

I was silent. And then I said, – She was shaking her head. I think she means this is a dead end.

After a while, Mimpriss said, – There are other places I can take you. There were nine murders in total, over about eight weeks.

She started playing with the cross around her neck, as Alexis had just done with her own imaginary necklace. And I thought, this couldn't be a coincidence.

– Are you a religious person? I said.

Mimpriss stopped playing with her cross and said, – You know this. Church in Wales.

– And you're a member of St Dyfrig's?

She nodded.

– So why didn't you know about the organ? It was broken months ago.

She looked down. – We were both in relationships. We used to use the church as an excuse to see each other, she said. – I haven't felt like going back since.

– Then I know exactly where to go.

8.30PM

I knew where it would be. You would have put it underneath the seat which is two from the middle on the first row of pews. I knew because this was my seat when I turned up late at Mum's funeral. Only I would know this. It would be the kind of fail-safe only you would do.

There were no tourists around. We walked up the steps. Inside, there were long white pillars reaching up to the high roof. Each window depicted a station of the cross. The walls themselves were stained wood, with a massive altar at the back.

But there was one problem.

There were no pews.

The middle of the church was empty. It was a wide open space with a stained wooden floor.

My footsteps echoed when I trod into the space. To the left of the altar, behind the pillars, was a stack of folded wooden chairs. I went up to them and looked around. There was no sign of a thesis.

I said, – I thought it would be under a pew.

Mimpriss said, – I wish you'd told me that was your grand idea. The church had them removed to bring in some revenue. You can get married here, have the reception, salsa lessons, all sorts.

We looked around the space but found nothing. Mimpriss said that there was a crypt underneath that had been turned into a cafe, so we headed back outside. But when we got into the fresh air, I felt something. So I asked Mimpriss for her purse and positioned it on the top step. Then I turned it forty-five degrees and stepped back.

Two men appeared in front of us, one about forty, and the other so old he could barely keep himself from falling over as he leant on a cane. The older man was wearing an old-fashioned curly wig, almost like a barrister, the hair tumbling past his shoulders. The younger man pointed at something on a piece of paper he was holding, then pointed at something in front of them that was above their head height. Then the elder man pointed, and they both laughed, and they were gone.

– Good gracious, Mimpriss said. – That was Steffan ab Gruffudd showing Iolo Morganwg how the building work was going on.

– It wasn't Alexis, though.

– One of those was the man who designed this church. I didn't expect to see them.

She felt for her necklace, rubbing it as she spoke.

I asked Mimpriss to point as the men did. I went back inside, and looked at the other side of the door. Above it on the inside wall was a large picture of the ascension. I got one of the stacked chairs, then stood on it and removed the picture. Behind it, on the other side, was a taped brown envelope.

After I called her back in to the church, I threw the envelope down to Mimpriss. Then I put the picture back as Mimpriss unsealed the envelope. She pulled out a stack of paper.

– What does it say on the front? I said, as I hopped down.

She read it out, word for word, including some sort of scribbled note. Then she passed the manuscript over to me. I flipped through it. No Lorem Ipsum, no Keep Safe Danger. I knew, finally, that this was the right one.

– Let's take a picture of every page, she said.

I looked at my phone as I got down. – Not enough time, I said, and started running, leaving Mimpriss behind.

8.45PM

By the time I had sprinted to Shields Square I was heaving and retching and my body felt ready to give up. I ran through the dark passage entrance, and saw Emily in the far corner next to the railings.

Her hands were clasped in front of her. Behind her stood the figure of Hurley. Behind Hurley and Emily stood Coburn and Radar.

No one said a word. I stayed at the mouth of the passage as they stared, waiting for me to get my breath back.

I figured I could tell them to let her go as I threw the thesis to the side so that Emily and I could escape down one of the passages. I stopped twenty feet shy. They were still silent. Coburn and Radar weren't even looking at me.

I have what you want, I said. – Let her go and I'll throw it over.

They all stayed staring straight ahead.

And then I realised why.

They disappeared. It was a loop.

I was in the square by myself. And then, ahead of me. I saw Hurley. He was leading a stream of people. To my right I saw Peter Blake Turner, also leading what looked like to be many people, all dressed smartly in suits and overcoats and dresses. I turned to run, but behind me I saw Coburn coming from the passage I'd come down and Radar from the other, each leading two dozen men and women, all staring.

They walked towards me. I tried to run but they blocked me from every direction. I found myself pinned to the corner spot where Hurley had shown me the old man's murder, the spot where Turner had failed to convert me to his cause, the place where I saw an innocent man strangled and slit and his innards dragged out by the very people now surrounding me.

I was, in a word, fucked.

8.50PM

There were a few elderly people in the crowd. A few others were wheezing. If I charged the weaker ones I could always hope for the best.

But before I had a chance, Radar and Coburn each came forward and grabbed one of my arms. I could feel them pumping where they gripped, where the blood was being stopped from circulating.

I could hear myself breathing heavily. And I wondered why. Everyone around me was silent. They were all staring at me. A man in a trilby was sneering, barely able to hide his contempt. Then Coburn let go of my arm and he stepped back. Radar stayed still, his grip tightening and making me wince.

Everyone turned to face Turner. He said, – And this marks the very spot where poor Thomas, or Twm to his friends, met his end. The Butcher, in this case, didn't hold back. Perhaps after being disturbed not an hour earlier when trying to murder a man called Alfred, the Butcher took his frustration out on Twm to such an extent that a policeman, on seeing Twm's mutilated body, was physically sick into the gutter.

As he was saying this, I felt a sharp point in my back, and Radar leant forward and whispered in my ear, – Move and I'll put this in all the way.

I stayed very still. I couldn't work out why the hell Turner was saying all this. Everyone present already knew what he was saying. But over their heads, I saw that another group of people had appeared at the other end of the square. The majority had blue backpacks, and a figure in the middle was holding up an umbrella. At least I was safe for a moment. Then when Peter Blake Turner was halfway through a sentence, he looked at two dark-haired young men with the blue backpacks, right at the back of his crowd and said, – I think you have the wrong tour group, sorry. That's yours, over there.

He pointed at the other group, and the two men apologised in Spanish accents and went to join them.

The Spiritists stayed silent. But after a couple of minutes, the tour group with the backpacks left, and with them my sense of hope.

Everyone turned to face Turner again. The knife in my back nearly pierced my skin and I didn't dare move.

– The Festival of the Ghost is upon us, Turner said. – And what a special one this promises to be.

He moved into the centre of the circle that had opened up where I was standing. He pulled out a single hair from his own head and twirled it in his fingers. The Butcher came out in front of us. I could feel the crowd's energy at seeing him, as if they had just seen a celebrity. The Butcher took a few steps forward as Turner got out of his way. Then he strained his arms and contorted himself in a strangling motion, but there was no one there and he had no one to kill.

– As you know, Turner said, walking in a slow circle, – The Butcher of Butetown, one of our most treasured ghosts, also has the potential to fade, like an old photograph. We must renew his victims to honour the Butcher so he may shine once more.

There was some shuffling from the crowd. Two people parted, and I heard the sounds of someone struggling. Emily came out, being held by Hurley. She had a gag over her mouth. He brought her out and held her next to me. I went to move but felt the knife once more against my skin.

– The past, Turner said, – is with us in the present.

Coburn clipped Emily at the back of her legs and she fell to her knees. Turner held a knife up to the crowd, then put it inside his coat. I was helpless. He put his hands around Emily's neck, and I felt myself urging my body to move, and Emily kicked but then the crowd started whispering and mumbling to each other, and Turner looked around. Hurley grabbed the top of Emily's head and pushed to the ground and told her to stay down.

I tried to see where Turner was looking.

A woman in a top hat had entered the square. She was holding up an umbrella. A long line of people followed her. The Spiritists had turned to look at her. The man in the trilby gave her a worse scowl than he had given me. She looked at the Spiritists as they walked forwards. Then she said, making herself stand straight so she could look over them to see Turner, – Oh, a re-enactment with the crowd. I'll have to up my game. Never mind, we won't get in your way, plenty of room. OK, my people. Gather round, fill in the gaps like the other group have, you know the drill. So in 1882, Shields Square, named after a local winner of the Victoria Cross at Rorke's Drift, is where the sock seller Thomas Marks found himself after coming out of a police cell at one thirty in the morning on the charge of being drunk and disorderly....

The woman talked on while Turner pretended to mumble something.

It would only be a minute or so before they left. I would have to do something big, something they wouldn't expect.

I thought of the way your loop looked at me and it felt like you could see me, the way Mum gave me a squeeze when I finally got to say goodbye, and that moment when Covey and Mimpriss hugged and were one. I thought back to the last time I was in this square, when Turner had released the old man who was put in to replace Thomas Marks, and how that old man, or ghost, had managed to claw his face.

I started strumming the insides of my fingers with my thumb. Then I angled my neck from side to side, and pushed the blade of Radar's knife into the skin of my own back; enough for me to find the balance I was looking for.

In front of me, the Butcher of Butetown came out. He was repeating the same movements as before, collar up, strangling someone who was no longer there.

Turner noticed first, then a few of the Spiritists looked around to make sure that the real Butcher tour led by the lady in the top hat hadn't noticed. As more and more people noticed the empty loop of strangulation being enacted simultaneously, I felt Radar's grip loosen. I had to take the chance.

I elbowed the knife away and heard it clatter. I threw my hand forward and found a path through to the Butcher. I pulled him out by the arm, and he looked at me with complete surprise. Then he glanced behind me and saw Coburn. It was as if he recognised him instantly. I felt the Butcher pass through me and I felt a chill, as if I had never felt that kind of rage before. Turning around, I saw the Butcher get to Coburn and slash with his knife across Coburn's throat.

The blood came spurting out, and then it started running down Coburn's neck. His hand went up and he felt the damp and pulled it away. His mouth opened, he dropped to his knees, his mouth opening and closing but no words coming out. He tried holding his throat together, white flesh pressing bruise colours. Radar ran over and started to take off his jacket, but the Butcher slashed again and got Radar in the aorta, his shirt going from white to deep red in an instant. Radar put the jacket around his own throat as Coburn gurgled and fell forward.

Everybody started running in different directions. The Butcher turned around.

They had all looped him countless times. And they had stolen his eternal victims.

I locked eyes with the Butcher. He took two steps towards me, his knife came up and I flinched, but his legs stayed still. He looked down and tried grabbing his own leg but it didn't move.

His legs were sinking. They were sinking into the ground. He started shouting and protesting as the ground got up to his waist, and finally his whole body was dragged under, and the Butcher was gone.

The woman in the top hat looked at me through the running people. She saw Coburn and Radar and the blood on the floor and she and her Butcher tour participants started running. And then I looked over at a small passage, and saw in between the chaos of running people that Hurley, knife in hand, was dragging Emily through it.

9PM

I was about to run after them when I felt a pair of eyes on me. I looked around and locked with Peter Blake Turner. He was running at me, and just as I realised that Turner must have seen that he was safe from the Butcher, he tackled me.

I felt like I had been torn in half. A bone at the top of my neck hit the ground first. But before I could check if I was OK, Turner rained down a haymaker on the side of my head, and followed it with another. I managed a weak punch, hooked an arm under his leg and got up.

He stood, and pulled out a knife from his inside pocket. He smiled. We both knew what bringing a knife to a fist fight meant.

But I knew that if he wasn't going to fight fair, then I didn't have to either.

I put my foot in Coburn's blood. Then I smeared my heel back and forth on the floor. Turner looked at what I was doing, and I coughed.

Turner's father came out in front of us. He was showing off his palm and smiling, and it was obvious that he was in front of a crowd.

Peter Turner looked on incredulously at his father. His knife came down for a second. In that time I found a path through and grabbed Turner Senior's tattooed hand and yanked him out.

Turner Junior shouted no, but it was too late.

Turner senior looked at me, horrified, then turned to his son. He tried grabbing his arms as Turner Junior started saying – No, no, no, but Turner Senior's feet were already under the ground. Slowly he was sucked under, as Turner Junior cried and tried to grab at him but then Turner Senior was gone.

I wasn't wasting my time while this was happening.

I had carefully pulled the knife I had stolen from Hurley's kitchen out of my jeans, and as soon as Turner Senior had gone I lunged forward.

I caught Turner Junior in the neck. The knife went in and stopped hard. I pulled it out and with it came blood and a rasping sound. Turner's hands came up to his neck, and he fell on the floor on his back.

I turned and ran, hoping Hurley hadn't taken Emily too far.

9.10PM

There were two Spiritists disappearing up the long narrow passage. But there was no struggle, and they were running, so it couldn't have been Hurley and Emily. I turned right, and ran down another passage that led to the main road, hoping that this was the route they took.

But there was no sign of them in either direction.

I closed my eyes and breathed out. Then I straightened my back, clicked my neck and opened my eyes.

They appeared in front of me. Hurley still had a hand up to Emily's back, indicating he had a knife held to her, but the gag was off her mouth. She was holding tight to the thesis. He looked both ways then nodded with his head for them to turn right, and they disappeared.

I followed to where it looked like they were going. It was in the direction of the campus. But when I got to the end of the street I stopped.

There would be no way Hurley would take her to such a public place. So I took a gamble, no time to check, and made my way to Hurley's street. I banged on his door, smoothed it down with my palm and they appeared in front of me. Hurley tapped the code in, opened his door, and he shoved her in.

I entered the code. But it seemed so obvious. If he took her here he would be trapped. Hurley had already mentioned not wanting to bring anything to his own front door. This situation would be no different.

He was obfuscating. He was using the loops against me.

I ran to the main road. There on the corner by a shop, I looked around as a car went past. I grabbed a crisp packet from the gutter and folded it over and laid it down.

Hurley and Emily appeared in front of me. He was still holding her at the shoulder, one hand still at her back, and shoving her. They rounded the corner to the left and started walking.

I knew where they were headed. There was only one place for them to go.

I marched down the street, and ran where the pavement and traffic of people allowed me to. When I could see the street corner ahead of me I started to smell smoke. Then I rounded the corner and saw that it was coming from the brown tiers of the Spirit Freedom Centre itself.

I sprinted and almost tripped up on a loose pavement slab that was being pushed upwards by one of the trees, and barged inside, ignoring the pain in my shoulder. The smoke was pouring out from the main hall. The door frame to the main hall itself was fierce with fire.

I heard coughing and shouting. I stepped forward towards the smoke. I kicked the door in and some of the pews were blazing. Emily was tied to the altar, the thesis by her side. I breathed in and braced myself. But then I felt a knock to the back of my head. The world started spinning and I found myself on the floor. I went blind for a second, but I could only half take notice in the pain.

I turned over, and stood above me, fire extinguisher in hand, was Hurley.

– Well, this is just perfect, he said. – Now I

don't have to track you down to destroy all of my connections.

I tried standing up, but Hurley kicked me under the chin and I went back down. I started to crawl but Hurley kicked me again. I rolled away and heard the fire extinguisher tonk down where my head had been.

I had neither the energy nor the balance to fight this battle. I needed a way out. So in the second I had, before the metal canister came down again, I rubbed my hands together and blew into them and let the breath go towards Hurley.

Out of nowhere between us came a stream of people leaving the main hallway doors. It must have been the end of a service. Everyone was smiling and even a young Peter Blake Turner walked past wearing shorts.

I stood up and threw my weight towards where I had last seen Hurley. I connected with him and tackled him and brought him down. He cracked his head on a wall as my face planted on the ground.

My nose was numb. There was blood dripping from it. I picked myself up.

Hurley was out cold. The people disappeared. I raced towards the door and tried to get in. I could hear no coughing now. I tried to walk through but the heat was too intense. The smoke making my eyes smart, I tried feeling for the extinguisher.

I limped outside and around the back. I saw the fire exit and tried barging into it but it didn't budge.

I couldn't let Emily die. It was bad enough knowing that there was nothing I could do to help you, Alexis.

But then a thought came to me. I knew how to act. But it would be the hardest thing I ever did.

I ran back around the front of the building and went inside. Hurley was still out cold. I took off his shoe and lined it up parallel to the wall. Then I blew some smoke away and coughed.

You were in front of me. You were by the door, walking forward, probably looking at the receptionist or for someone to talk to, perhaps the first time you ever went into the Spirit Freedom Centre. Before you disappeared I grabbed you by the hand and pulled you towards me, and you were free.

You were looking at me, and then you smiled, and you stepped forward to give me a hug, but I stopped you. There was nothing I wanted to do more in that moment than hug you and tell you how much I missed you. But I raised my hand up and told you to stop. Then I pointed behind us. I had no idea if you would hear what I was about to say.

– Go help Emily, I said. – She needs you right now. I'll see you round the back. Your face went white. You turned, and ran through the door frame.

I ran to the fire exit. A second passed, and then another. I prayed that you hadn't been dragged away.

I was just about to go around the front again when the door opened. Smoke poured out and Emily fell into my arms. She dropped the thesis on the floor and was coughing. Her eyes were closed but there was water running from them. I tried speaking to her but she didn't answer. I looked up. Through the smoke I saw you smiling at me. You looked sad but happy. I laid Emily on the ground and stood up, but you smiled some more and walked back into the smoke and were gone.

5 JUNE

2PM

I was waiting in the wings. Lucky they didn't want to dress me up like a merchant of Venice like the others collecting PhD certificates, but I was feeling uncomfortable anyhow, being as I was unaccustomed to wearing a suit. A woman with a security lanyard nudged me, and I looked over to the stage. The Dean was stood there, also suited, and behind her were three rows of professors and dons, each one dressed more elaborately than the last, as if they were about to discuss what to do about the marauders from the Barbary Coast.

The Dean waited for everyone to quieten down again and said, – We have one more somewhat special award before we finish the postgraduates. It's a posthumous one. But after a troubling period for the history department, I'm delighted to award the title of Doctor of Philosophy to a former student taken away before her time. This award will be accepted on her behalf by her brother, Levi Silva. His sister, Alexis Silva, was an incredibly promising student whose work, as I'm sure you've heard, will change the face of how we interpret history for a long time to come.

The Dean looked in my direction. A huge roar came from the crowd. Many got to their feet, and the rest followed. I walked forward into the wall of sound. I nodded at the Dean, as I had been instructed, and accepted the certificate. Then as I walked off I turned to the professors and saw Jayne Mimpriss smiling at me. As I got to the end of the stage – praying that I wouldn't fall off – I looked up and saw Emily, clapping her hands as hard as she could, though not whooping and cheering like so many of the others.

But they weren't cheering for me. I could see it in Emily's face, in the way she smiled, with the sadness that sometimes overwhelmed her as she tried to hold it together. All of this was for you. Not that I didn't get anything out of the moment. Because this is how we said goodbye. Or goodbye for now, at least. Because I knew, at some point, we would see each other again, and that is something I will forever be holding on to.

ACKNOWLEDGEMENTS

Thank you Emma, for strolling around streets for hours upon hours on various walking tours with me / for keeping me company while we try to capture the atmosphere of an obscure street / for just being you.

Thank you Gwen, for taking a gamble on me, going back as far as NWR 100, I will be forever grateful for how you have helped me and also that we share a similar sense of humour.

Thank you Rich, for publishing this, Parthian have been very good to me.

Thank you Susie, for your guidance and also how you have helped me grow as a writer.

A New Welsh Writing Awards winner, originally created by *New Welsh Review*.

NEW WELSH RAREBYTE

Special thanks are due from the publishers to Richard Powell, our philanthropic sponsor in the New Welsh Writing Awards manuscript prize, which has greatly benefited from this ongoing generous annual support.

PARTHIAN A CARNIVAL OF VOICES

Woman Who Brings the Rain
A Memoir of Hokkaido, Japan
Eluned Gramich
With original calligraphic art by Kuniko Sheldon

'Most rewarding... suits perfectly the changing boundaries of our modern world'
– Wales Arts Review

My Oxford
A Memoir
Catherine Haines

'This powerful, thought-provoking debut explores the author's experiences of her eating disorder in a narrative that is emotionally and intellectually complex yet unflinchingly accessible.'
– Frank Egerton

Earwitness
A Search for Sonic Understanding in Stories
Ed Garland

'Intriguing, funny, learned, thoughtful and moving'
– Niall Griffiths

MANDY SUTTER
BUSH MEAT

'...wonderfully tempered... elevating, touching, darkly humane'
– ALISON MOORE, author of the Booker Prize shortlisted *The Lighthouse*

NEW WELSH RAREBYTE

PARTHIAN A CARNIVAL OF VOICES

ANNA and the ANGEL
ELEANOR WILLIAMS

SLATE HEAD
THE ASCENT OF BRITAIN'S SLATE-CLIMBING SCENE
PETER GOULDING

Birdsplaining
A Natural History
JASMINE DONAHAYE

FESTIVAL OF THE GHOST
JOÃO MORAIS

NEW WELSH RAREBYTE